WYATT

Seven Brides for Seven Soldiers - Book 4

LYNN RAYE HARRIS

The Hostile Operations Team® and Lynn Raye Harris® are trademarks of H.O.T. Publishing, LLC.

Printed in the United States of America

First Printing, 2017

For rights inquires, visit www.LynnRayeHarris.com

WYATT
Copyright © 2017 by Lynn Raye Harris
Cover Design Copyright © 2017 Damonza

ISBN: 978-1-941002-26-1

Seven Brides for Seven Soldiers

Fall in love with seven sexy and irresistible soldiers who find their courage and heart tested like never before in the battle for love! This multi-author collaborative series of contemporary romance novels is brought to you by best-selling authors Barbara Freethy, Roxanne St. Claire, Christie Ridgway, Lynn Raye Harris, Julia London, Cristin Harber and Samantha Chase. You won't want to miss a single one!

Ryder (#1) - Barbara Freethy
Adam (#2) - Roxanne St. Claire
Zane (#3) - Christie Ridgway
Wyatt (#4) - Lynn Raye Harris
Jack (#5) - Julia London
Noah (#6) - Cristin Harber
Ford (#7) - Samantha Chase

Prologue

Wyatt Chandler straightened his Navy dress uniform collar and took a deep breath. He didn't want to walk into that church, didn't want to see the casket of his teammate with the American flag draped on top. Mostly he didn't want to see Danny's wife and baby girl. He didn't want Lisa to see the guilt in his eyes.

Guilt because he hadn't been able to save Danny from the sniper's bullet that had ended his life. Wyatt shoved a hand through his hair, which was cropped short in proper military style for a change, and sucked in another breath.

"Just get in there, dammit, and do your duty," he muttered.

He shoved the door open and walked into the church. It was darker than he'd expected. It was overcast outside, and the meager light coming through the stained-glass windows cast a muted glow on everything.

But of course it was gloomy. Candles flickered, but they couldn't replace the light the world had lost when it lost Danny.

Wyatt stopped in the back of the church and took

everything in. The gloom. The sobbing. The sadness. The utter despair of a life cut too short and the pain of those who had to go onward. The little girl playing down front who was too small to understand what was really happening and why her daddy was never coming home again.

A lump formed in his throat. His eyes stung. He'd sat through a funeral when he was not much older than Danny's little girl. He didn't remember much about it, but he remembered Gran sobbing while Gramps sat with his arm around her and tried to tell her it would be okay.

But it could never be okay. She'd lost her son and daughter-in-law. Wyatt and Gramps were all she'd had left.

Now it was only Wyatt because Gramps had died two years ago. The sobbing down front grew louder, and Wyatt clamped his jaw tight at the anguish in it.

If he stayed in the Navy, would he go home in a casket too? Would Gran have to sit through another funeral, sobbing her heart out like Danny's family was doing?

Soon he was going to have to make a decision about his future. But not today. Today was about honoring Danny and about learning to live with this guilt that was eating him up inside.

He strode down the aisle toward the flag-draped casket. He was here to pay his respects. One last time.

Chapter 1

Four months later…

WYATT SLID into the booth at No Man's Land, a diner located on a portion of the Sentinel Bridge, and picked up the menu even though he didn't really need it. The HALO pancakes topped with snow and drowned in rocket fuel were his favorite item on the breakfast menu. A former Navy SEAL, he'd done enough HALO jumps out of airplanes over enemy territory to get quite the kick out of pancakes named after what was essentially a very risky venture.

"Hi, Wyatt. How's it going this morning?"

Mandy stood there with her order pad and a pen, smiling at him with that pretty smile of hers. He thought he should feel a hint of interest in her, but he didn't. He should probably worry about that, especially since he'd been out of the SEALs for nearly two months now and had yet to kiss a woman—much less spend the night with one—but he couldn't bring himself to care.

In truth, he had a hard time caring about much of anything right now. Except Gran, of course. Gran, who was at her doctor's appointment and refused to let him join her. When he'd dropped her off, she'd told him to go get some breakfast and stop skulking around.

"Pretty good," he said with a smile and a wink. "How about you?"

"I'm okay."

She said it shyly, and he wondered if she was sweet on him or something. He hoped not, because he was so not the kind of man for a girl like her. Innocent. Nice. Probably naïve.

She cleared her throat. "Do you know what you want or should I just get you some coffee first and come back?"

He handed her the plastic menu. "I'll take the pancakes and some coffee. And a side of scrambled eggs."

"Sounds great. I'll be back with your coffee. Food will be up soon."

Wyatt knew from experience that he was about to get a lot of food. But he'd been doing manual labor off and on for Garrison Construction the past few weeks, so he wasn't worried about an expanding waistline. Construction wasn't the same as humping through the jungle in full ruck, but it was still pretty hard work. It was also satisfying, like when he'd helped Adam Tucker turn the boathouse into a camp dorm over at A To Z Watersports.

The door opened and Zane Tucker, Adam's twin, wandered in. He lifted his chin when he saw Wyatt and made his way over, flopping down on the bench opposite.

"How's it hanging this morning, Wyatt?"

Wyatt raised an eyebrow. Ever since Zane had gotten cozy with the town librarian, Miss Harper Grace, he'd been smiling more. He was smiling now, matter of fact, and while it grated on Wyatt somewhere deep down, he was also happy for his friend. Zane was the jokester of their group—they didn't call him Insane Zane for nothing—but Wyatt had always thought the joking hid deeper feelings of inadequacy. Maybe because Zane had been sickly as a child.

Well, he wasn't sickly now. If anything, he was radiating health and happiness.

"It's hanging. Lower than yours."

Zane snorted. "Asshole. I'm still not sure I've forgiven you for the Wonder Woman costume. You aren't working very hard to get back on my good side either."

"I'm still on your good side. Without me, you might never have admitted you love Harper."

"Oh, I definitely would have. Without the costume though."

Wyatt flicked a gaze at the Snake River flowing below them. Eagle's Ridge was beautiful this time of year. The foliage was lush, the river rolled against the banks, bringing water sports and good fishing, and the Blue Mountains soared against a clear sky.

Danny would have loved it here. He was crazy for good fishing. He'd told Wyatt all about his family farm and the bass ponds there while they were high up in the Hindu Kush, searching for insurgents and tracking down a terrorist leader. They'd survived that mission, just like they'd survived so many others.

Until one day when it all went wrong.

"What's the bug up your ass this morning?" Zane asked, frowning.

Wyatt didn't answer because Mandy chose that moment to return with the coffee.

"Hey, Zane—you want some coffee?"

"Sure thing. And give me the Two NCOs with Train

Tracks," he added, ordering the scrambled eggs and bacon. "Add some hash browns too."

"Be right up," Mandy said as she jotted on her order pad. A few seconds later she was back with a second coffee cup.

When she left this time, Zane took a sip and waited. He clearly hadn't forgotten his question or Wyatt's silence.

"There's no bug," Wyatt said, knowing Zane wouldn't give up. They were too close for lies, so Wyatt went with evasion instead. "How's Harper?"

"Nice try. She's fine, by the way. But you aren't. We've all noticed it."

Wyatt's gut twisted. "Why would you say that? I'm exactly where I want to be, doing what I want to do. I'm the definition of fine."

"You've been in town for almost two months, and all you do is the occasional construction project for the Garrisons or odd jobs for whoever gives you something to do."

"I spent a solid week pasting photos into Gran's albums, don't forget. Gave myself a paper cut."

Zane wasn't fooled by the attempt at humor. "What's going on with you, Wyatt?"

Wyatt's hand tightened on the mug. "I'm fine, Zane."

"Yeah, but you left the SEALs—and you won't tell any of us why."

Wyatt kicked back as if he were the most relaxed guy in the world. "It was time, that's all. Gran's sick. She needs me—"

"That woman does not need you, bro. She hasn't slowed down a bit since her diagnosis. About all I've noticed is she doesn't stop at the bakery for donuts anymore. Type 2 diabetes isn't a death sentence. It's controllable with medication and diet, and she's doing just that." Zane leaned forward, elbows on the table. "So what really gives, huh?"

Wyatt hesitated for a long moment. But his pain was his alone. He wasn't going to burden his friends with any of it. Ryder, Adam, and Zane were happier than he'd ever seen them. He didn't know about Jack, couldn't get him to commit to anything more than a few phone calls, but he suspected Jack was dealing with something serious of his own. Then there was Noah, who was handling family shit, and Ford, who seemed determined to stay on the other side of the country even though his family wanted him home and had a construction company for him to run.

Nope, nobody needed to listen to his shit, so he wasn't going to talk about it.

"Nothing, man. I'm just tired. I saw a lot overseas, a lot of bad stuff…" He hesitated. "Gran is the only family I have left. I thought I should come home and be around for her."

Zane's gaze searched his. He could tell the moment his friend decided to quit digging. Knowing Zane, however, it was only a temporary reprieve.

"Fine. But what do you plan to do with yourself in the long run? You're too young to retire, and you need more than odd jobs here and there to keep you alive."

Wyatt shook his head and grinned. "I saved a lot of combat pay. I'm good for a long time to come."

Zane didn't seem convinced. "I'm glad you won't be panhandling or anything, but I still think you need to find your calling. Whatever that is."

The food arrived then, and Wyatt's mouth started to water at the sight of all those pancakes. Nobody made pancakes like these. Not only that, but Sam Tucker's home-made maple syrup was the taste of Wyatt's childhood in a bite.

Zane tore into his eggs and bacon, and Wyatt forked up a bite of fluffy pancakes before meeting his friend's eyes again.

"It's cool, Zane. I have some ideas, but I'm not ready to jump on any of them yet." It was a lie, but Zane didn't need to know that.

Zane nodded. "Let me know if I can help. When you're ready."

"I definitely will. You owe me a few."

"Pretty sure you owe *me* after the Wonder Woman incident."

After breakfast, they parted ways. Zane returned to A To Z, and Wyatt shoved his hands in his pockets and walked back to his truck. It was still a good half hour before he had to pick up Gran. He leaned against the truck, one leg crossed over the other, and studied the picture the mountains and river made.

Eagle's Ridge was beautiful. The scenery was practically the only thing that gave him any measure of comfort these days. When you stood beneath mountains so glorious, your troubles didn't seem nearly as big as you thought they were.

His cell phone buzzed in his pocket. He slid it out and glanced at the screen. It was a Maryland number, but not one he recognized. He thought about letting it go to voice mail in case it was a telemarketer or something, but since he had time to kill he decided to answer.

"Hey, Wyatt. This is Hawk," a voice said in response to his clipped greeting.

Wyatt blinked. Hawk, whose real name was Jack Hunter, had been a legendary sniper in the Hostile Operations Team, the special terrorist-hunting unit Wyatt had been a member of for the past three years. Hawk had left HOT to start his own security firm protecting high-end clients like his wife, pop superstar Gina Domenico. Wyatt had met the man a couple of times but didn't really know him.

"Hey, Hawk. What can I do for you?"

"I understand you've left the unit," the other man said. "And I was wondering if you'd like to put your special skills to use."

Special skills was code for the ability—and willingness—to use lethal force in a variety of ways. Wyatt frowned as he gazed at the mountains. There was a peak up there where the eagles nested that gave the town its name. He hadn't been up there in years. He really needed to go see it again...

"I don't think so," he said. "But I appreciate the offer."

"You haven't even heard the offer yet," Hawk replied. He sounded amused rather than annoyed.

"Yeah, well, I gotta tell you the truth—I think I'd be tempted. And I don't want to be."

Because yeah, he *did* miss the high-octane thrill of operations. He missed the adrenaline rush, the highs of a job done well. He missed being a SEAL, and he missed HOT, a place where only the best of the best gained entrance.

Still, he'd made his decision. He was done.

"Look, it's pretty simple really," Hawk continued. "I have a client who needs guarding in Eagle's Ridge. Nothing more complicated than that. You interested?"

He didn't want to be. He really didn't. But he could listen, right?

"You have my attention."

Chapter 2

"Hey, Wyatt, what's up?"

Wyatt looked up. He was standing in the two-story airport terminal, waiting for the last flight from Seattle for the day, and wondering how he'd let himself be talked into this gig.

"Waiting for flight 22," he said to Ryder Westbrook, who didn't quite hide his frown fast enough.

Shit, were all his friends talking about him behind his back? Probably. He hadn't told any of them he was leaving the Navy. He'd just shown up one day and announced it. At least he'd gotten to share the flight into town with Ford, who hadn't asked too many questions.

Wyatt had told them all he'd come home to be near Gran, and he thought they'd all accepted it. Clearly they hadn't.

"Who's on flight 22?" Ryder asked.

"My next job."

Ryder blinked. "A job?"

"Yeah. Some reality show star who's acquired an

obsessed fan. She's coming here to get away from Seattle for a while."

"Sounds interesting."

Wyatt folded his arms over his chest and glanced out the windows. A plane was coming in for a landing. Must be the one.

"Not really," he said.

"But you took the job."

He shrugged. "Couldn't refuse the pay."

Ryder looked confused. "Thought you had all that combat pay saved up?"

Yeah, his friends had been talking about him. Wyatt had only mentioned the combat pay to Zane this morning. It hadn't come up before because nobody'd asked. And now Ryder knew, which meant he and Zane—and Adam, probably—were playing telephone tag.

"I do. But money's money."

Which Ryder would know, coming from the rich side of town. He'd always been the golden boy, the heir to the Westbrook fortune, and he understood instinctively the value of a dollar. Wyatt knew his friend was more compli- cated than that, and that he'd struggled with the expecta- tions of his family. Still, Ryder didn't know what it was like to fear losing his home or his savings.

"True. So what show is she from?"

"*American Princess.*"

Ryder shook his head. "Never heard of it."

"Me neither. Apparently it's a thing though." He jerked his head at the plane as it touched down on the runway. "This girl is the catty one everybody hates. Or so I've been told."

"You don't know? I'd have thought you'd Google her as soon as you took the job."

"The security firm sent over a dossier. There were no

clips of the show. Besides, I had to hang shelves for Hildie Fontana. Damn woman talked so much it took three times as long as it should have. I barely escaped."

Ryder burst out laughing. "Damn, dude. How'd you get roped into doing anything for Hildie? You know she can't stop talking. How she manages to collect any gossip when she never shuts up long enough to listen is a mystery to me."

Wyatt agreed. "Gran told her I'd do it. I couldn't say no after that."

"So who's cheating on who this week?"

"Couldn't say. I tuned her out."

Ryder clapped a hand on his shoulder and squeezed. "Smart man. Hey, as much as I want to see this TV star of yours, I gotta get out of here. Promised Bailey I'd be home on time tonight."

"Tell her I said hi."

"I will. Talk to you later."

Ryder strolled away, and Wyatt went back to watching the gate. He knew what Paige Spencer looked like, thanks to the dossier Hawk had sent him. She was five-two, blond, and able to convey her superiority with a single arched eyebrow. The production stills from *American Princess* were illuminating in that regard.

She was the daughter of Greg Spencer, the founder and co-owner of SpenTech, a firm that built specialized circuit boards for aircraft. Spencer had a house in Eagle's Ridge, a fishing retreat a few miles out of town that sat on a spectacular curve in the river. It would be easy to take Paige there and wait while the police sorted out her crazed-fan situation in Seattle, but Wyatt didn't trust the easy way. No, he was taking her up the mountain and staying in a vacation rental cabin there until he got the all clear.

Hawk had agreed it was the best plan. He'd made the

arrangements to rent the place and get Wyatt the equipment he needed to monitor their surroundings. All he had to do now was collect Paige Spencer and drive her up there.

Wyatt crossed his arms and legs and leaned against the wall, waiting as the plane taxied up to the terminal. There was no jet bridge yet, though as the new airport owner, Ryder was working on that during his expansion. The passengers had to walk down a set of stairs that were rolled up to the aircraft and then up another set of stairs to get inside the terminal. It was curious that Paige Spencer was flying commercial when her daddy most certainly had a jet of his own. Probably several.

But hey, rich people. Who knew why they did what they did?

Wyatt didn't have too long to wait. Passengers started to emerge from the gate area, rolling wheeled bags or carrying backpacks. Some were returning residents, others were tourists. They got a lot of tourists throughout the summer. Folks started coming around Founders' Day in March and kept on coming until the first snow fell. Even then, Eagle's Ridge had enough winter activities to keep people coming in, though in fewer numbers.

The flood of passengers turned to a trickle. Wyatt frowned and took out his phone. He had no messages from Hawk. No notice that the plan had changed.

He waited a few more minutes. Just when he was ready to dial Hawk, a small blond woman emerged. She looked pissed too. Behind her, a hulking man carried a pink pet carrier.

Shit.

Just what he needed, some yappy-ass dog barking at every sound and movement that happened over the next few days. He pictured a Chihuahua—tiny, barky, and wearing a jeweled collar—that Miss Paige Spencer would cuddle and coo a raft of nonsense to.

Why had he agreed to this again?

Oh yeah, he liked money. And, truth be told, he was starting to get a little bored. Not that he didn't like working with his hands and building things, but he'd spent so many years fighting to stay alive in the face of danger that anything else started to seem a little surreal after a while.

He pushed away from the wall and strode toward the pint-sized blonde. She had a look of utter determination on her face. Her hair bounced as she walked. He let his gaze slide down her body.

Curves everywhere. Killer curves. She wore a skintight red dress beneath a black blazer with the sleeves shoved to her elbows and a pair of sky-high heels that looked more than painful. Maybe those shoes were the source of her sour look.

Still, she was pretty. Gorgeous, actually. He didn't have much experience with TV or movie stars, but she looked like she fit right in with everything he'd ever seen about Hollywood.

She glided to a stop as he stepped in her path. She was a little thing, but she didn't even miss a beat. "Move it, or I'll make Bruce move you."

Wyatt didn't know whether to laugh or snort in derision. He opted for returning her arched brow with one of his own. He'd faced down worse than her.

"Sorry, sweetheart, but I'm your ride while you're in town."

Bruce stood behind her, grinning almost gleefully. Wyatt didn't have time to wonder because the instant Paige turned her glare on the man, his face went blank.

"Your father arranged a security escort for you, Miss Spencer. I'm headed back to Seattle on the next flight."

So she hadn't known that little bit of information. Judging by the way her body stiffened, she wasn't happy about it either.

Well, neither was he. There were other ways to earn money.

Except, with Gran's diabetes, Wyatt didn't know when he might need an influx of cash to help care for her. The more he could save, the better. She wouldn't take a dime from him right now—he'd tried—but she might need it eventually.

"Are you even planning to ask him for identification?" Paige asked Bruce, her voice dripping with derision. "Or did you plan on handing me over and hightailing it back to the aircraft?"

Wyatt didn't like her tone, but he admired her thought process. One point for Miss Paige Spencer.

"I don't need identification, Miss Spencer. He matches the photo the security agency sent over. Name's Wyatt Chandler, and he's qualified."

Wyatt slid his wallet from his pocket and pulled out his driver's license. "Here," he said, holding it out to Paige, knowing she wouldn't be settled until she saw it for herself. She snatched it and studied the information. Then she lifted her pretty green-brown eyes and studied him.

A moment later, she handed the license back. Then she snapped her fingers at Bruce, who stepped forward and held out the pink pet carrier. At first, Wyatt was too bemused by the whole thing to even realize that Bruce was holding it for him.

But then it jarred into his brain that Paige had just treated both him and this Bruce guy like the hired help.

And maybe they were the hired help, but he wasn't *that* kind of help.

"Sorry, I'm allergic," he lied. "You'll have to carry it yourself."

Paige's brows drew together. "Mr. Fluffypants weighs twenty pounds."

Mr. Fluffypants?

"Then put him on a leash and walk him to the car. But I'm not carrying him."

"He doesn't walk on a leash."

"What the hell kind of dog doesn't walk on a leash?" Wyatt demanded.

This time her eyebrows climbed her forehead. Bruce turned the cage so Wyatt could get a good look at the animal inside.

A giant cat blinked back at him with blue eyes that said he was clearly superior to anything in this room. Hell, possibly in this state. The cat had long silver- and cream-colored fur. He was a gorgeous cat.

But he was also a *cat.* Wyatt didn't care for cats a whole lot. They were cold and superior for the most part. But then again, so was this cat's owner.

"Mr. Fluffypants is a *cat,*" Paige said with a sniff. "And I can't carry his cage and this purse too."

Her purse was at least half as big as she was. He never understood what women carried in those things, but apparently they needed a lot of room for it.

"Then I suggest you get a luggage cart," Wyatt told her.

Bruce was biting his lip and trying not to laugh. Wyatt wanted to shake the man and ask him why the hell he put up with this girl's crap. She was rich, sure, but that was no reason to take her shit.

Bruce set the cat carrier down and backed away as Paige turned to him. Clearly, she was planning to order him to take Mr. Fluffypants to Wyatt's truck. Bruce knew it as well as he did.

"Sorry, Miss Spencer, but I gotta be on that flight. Your father wants me back tonight. There's no time to spare."

After he turned and headed back down the steps, Paige whirled, her long hair swirling around her shoulders like a shampoo commercial. Her eyes were wide, her lips pink and glistening.

Damn, she was pretty.

"Who's going to help me get all my things to the car?"

"Like I said, you need a luggage cart. I'll watch the cat while you get one."

Chapter 3

Paige stared at the impossibly tall, broad, and extremely handsome man standing across from her like he was some kind of gunslinger—feet spread, arms dangling at his sides like he was about to quick draw on her, catlike reflexes primed and ready to explode—and felt a wave of despair crash over her.

It had been a long day. First, the network had announced the show was going on hiatus for the foreseeable future. She'd been *this close* to signing a deal to manufacture her own line of clothing—a deal her father had nothing to do with—and the company backed out when the show's prospects changed. If there was no *American Princess*, then where would she showcase her designs?

Without that guaranteed exposure, Hardy Manufacturing felt the venture was too risky. Paige had literally gone from a meeting in which she was about to shake hands on contract negotiations to sitting alone in the restaurant when one of the executives got a call from a friend at the studio.

They'd known the fate of the show before she had. It

still grated, especially since she'd had her dream in her grasp. The show was merely the vehicle to get her where she wanted to go—but now the vehicle not only had a flat tire, it might very well have blown an engine too.

As if her day couldn't get any worse, Paige had discovered a new letter from the man who called himself her biggest fan in her pile of mail. She was used to weird fan mail, but getting it at her home was alarming enough that she'd called the studio. They'd gotten the police involved, her father had stepped in, and now here she was in Nowheresville.

Wyatt William Chandler—according to his driver's license—was tall, sexy, and taciturn. He didn't display even an ounce of pity in those amber eyes. He truly expected her to get a luggage cart and load Mr. Fluffypants onto it. Then he probably thought she'd slip over to baggage claim and get her own suitcases while he watched. Did he expect her to load them into his car as well?

Anger roared through her. This was *not* how an employee was supposed to behave. She was tired and upset. She wanted a hot shower and a bed.

But this man insisted on being difficult in a day of difficulties. She wanted to fly at him—but it would get her nowhere. He was stronger than she was, and he didn't look inclined to respond to her fury.

Paige sucked in a deep breath. Let it out.

Sucked in another. Let it out.

She pasted on a smile. It shook at the edges. "I'll pay you two hundred dollars to get the cart and load everything for me. Cash money. You don't even have to report it to my father."

His frown deepened. A muscle at the corner of his jaw flexed. A prickle of alarm began to tingle in her belly.

"A thousand," she said before he could speak. "Surely

that's enough incentive."

"No." One word, clipped and angry.

Paige blinked. What was she missing here? In her experience, people wanted to be paid. Name the right price, and most people would do what you asked. It was tiring in a way, but it worked. She'd learned that lesson early in life, and she'd never been wrong.

Wyatt Chandler's eyes blazed hot as he glared at her. His nostrils flared and she thought he might be on the verge of losing his temper. She shot a glance over her shoulder, hoping beyond hope that Bruce might have returned, but of course he had not.

When she met Wyatt's gaze again, his brows were drawn low over those stormy hot eyes. He stalked past her and picked up Mr. Fluffypants.

Apparently, he *could* be bought. Somehow, that disappointed her.

But then he opened his mouth.

"Get this straight, Miss Spencer—I'm here to protect you, not fetch and carry for you. Ask nicely, and I'll help you every time. But I don't take bribes and I damned sure don't respond to haughty looks and snapping fingers from pampered princesses who think they're better than everyone else. Got it?"

"I wasn't bribing you," she protested. "I was bartering for a service. There is a difference."

"Come on," he growled, turning on his heel and striding off. Paige hurried to keep up, scooting along in her Louboutins faster than she'd thought possible. They were pinching her feet, but she didn't dare slow down to slip her flats from her bag. Not that she expected Wyatt Chandler would get away from her. She'd never been to Eagle's Ridge, but if the airport was anything to go by, it wasn't precisely a large metropolis.

More like Podunk, USA. Daddy liked to fish and hunt, and he'd bought a retreat here. She didn't like any of those things. She liked food delivery, spas and salons, shopping, and culture. Therefore, she'd never visited Eagle's Ridge. Daddy said they had winter sports, but she'd rather go to Aspen or Tahoe. Not to mention, she wasn't going to be locked up with Melanie, Daddy's third wife, for *any* length of time if she could help it.

Paige was winded by the time she caught up to Wyatt at baggage claim. The only suitcases still spinning around on the small carousel were hers. He set Mr. Fluffypants down and retrieved a luggage cart.

"I'm assuming those fancy things are yours."

"Yes."

He stacked the two Louis Vuitton suitcases on the cart, put Mr. Fluffypants on top, and started pushing the cart toward the door. Paige followed wearily. He crossed the parking lot to a very large and shiny black truck with four doors.

"Go ahead and get in," he told her as he unlocked it.

Paige thought about putting on her flats again, but vanity won out. Besides, she'd already walked a mile in the damned heels, and now she was about to sit down. She opened the door and climbed inside, arranging herself on the seat. The interior was big, like the man. She didn't think she'd ever ridden in a pickup truck before.

Wyatt loaded everything and shut the door. The instant he did so, Mr. Fluffypants started meowing. After all his silence throughout the trip, Paige was almost shocked to hear his kitty voice.

"It's okay, sweetie," she said. "Mama's taking you somewhere safe."

Wyatt returned from where he'd gone to take the cart

back, flipping his keys on his finger, and climbed inside. He turned whiskey eyes on her, frowning hard.

"Jesus, that cat is loud. Can't you shut him up?"

Paige's protective instincts flared. "He's been cooped up for hours and it's still not over. He's probably hungry and needs to pee. No, I can't shut him up."

Wyatt regarded her evenly. "Then I guess we need to get him where he can do those things."

"Yes, that would be nice. Thank you."

The streets were dark by now, so Paige couldn't see anything of the scenery. Not that she wanted to. She imagined it was mostly wide, empty spaces with wild animals lurking around every tree and rock. She knew there was a town, but Wyatt didn't take her through it. He drove down a dark road, his headlights cutting through the inky night.

Once, a deer lifted its head as they drove by. Paige squeaked. She'd never seen a deer in real life.

Wyatt glanced over at her and her cheeks heated. Yes, she was definitely the city mouse visiting the country. It was bound to be entertaining for him over the next few days. Or maybe just annoying.

"Tell me about your fan," Wyatt said, and her heart throttled into a higher gear.

"There's nothing to tell. The letters started coming after the sixth episode of *American Princess*. I assume you've seen the letters?"

"Yes."

"The most recent one arrived at my apartment this afternoon. Did you see that one?"

"I haven't, but I heard he sent a picture of you leaving the building that was taken this morning."

"Yes." Paige's fingers trembled as she smoothed them over her dress. That had been downright terrifying. "He wants me to know he can get to me."

22

"I'd say you're right about that. Did anything happen on the show that could have made him mad?"

The police had asked her the same thing. It was comforting in a way to know that Wyatt Chandler thought like the police did. That meant he had experience, unlike the bodyguard the studio had hired to accompany her to appearances. A man had walked right up to her at one of them and lifted her in his arms before her protector could react. Needless to say, he hadn't lasted. He'd been fired the next morning—and the man who'd picked her up was arrested and later let go.

He'd been investigated at the time, according to the lead detective in charge of her case. It was unlikely he was sending the letters, but they'd check him out again just in case. At the time, they'd determined he was just a college kid who'd been acting on a dare from his friends.

"In the last episode of *American Princess*, I had a date with Donnie Warren—he's an up-and-coming actor. It was staged, as so much of the show is. But King didn't like it." Her fan called himself King and her his queen. She hated it. "He took it seriously. He thinks we're destined to be together, so he accused me of cheating on him. He, uh, threatened to kidnap and torture Mr. Fluffypants to teach me a lesson."

Wyatt's fingers flexed on the steering wheel. "He threatened your cat?"

Paige swallowed a knot of tears. She could take a lot of vitriol directed at her—but to threaten Mr. Fluffypants? *No.*

"Yes." A single tear escaped to slide down her cheek. She dashed it away before he could see it. But he knew somehow.

His voice was hard and soothing at the same time. "Don't worry, Miss Spencer. I won't let the son of a bitch anywhere near you… *or* your cat."

Chapter 4

She was trying not to cry. Wyatt could tell that much in the dim lights from the dashboard. He'd seen her swipe a hand over her cheek and guessed that's what was going on. He'd also heard it in her voice.

She might be a pampered princess with a bit of a superiority complex, but she clearly loved her cat. She didn't deserve what was happening to her right now. Stalkers were the worst kinds of cowards. They got off on creating fear in their victims. They hid behind anonymous threats and stayed in the shadows, ratcheting up the tension to unbearable levels.

Sometimes they attacked. It wasn't a guarantee that Paige's stalker would do that, but it wasn't a chance anyone wanted to take either. According to Hawk, the police had a suspect. A man who'd worked as a temporary hire for *American Princess*. He'd been fired when he'd been caught stealing, and he'd threatened to ruin the show with behind-the-scenes knowledge. It was possible that he'd turned to threatening the show's star instead.

Wyatt had told her he wasn't letting anyone harm her

or her cat, and he meant it. The damned thing hadn't stopped squalling since they'd left the airport. Wyatt really hoped it shut up once they reached their destination.

It occurred to him there was no litter box where he was taking them. He hadn't known she was bringing a cat, so he hadn't prepared for it. Freaking hell.

He could turn around and head back to town, or he could call a friend. He chose the second option, disconnecting his phone from the truck's Bluetooth before doing so. He didn't need Paige to hear the other half of the conversation.

"Hey, Wyatt," Adam Tucker said. "Heard you got a job protecting an *American Princess.*"

Wyatt wanted to roll his eyes and laugh at the same time. Zane was the practical joker of their group, but Adam never missed a shot when he got one.

"Yeah, taking her up the mountain right now. Can you do me a favor?"

"I'll try. What do you need?"

"A litter box for a cat and some litter. A *big* cat."

As if on cue, Mr. Fluffypants let out a pissed-off yowl. And why wouldn't he be pissed with a name like that?

"Whoa, you sure that's not a tiger?"

"Not really. Can you do it?"

"Hang on…" Wyatt heard a muffled conversation that was probably Adam talking to Jane, the woman he'd fallen for shortly after Wyatt got back to town. He liked Jane. She was good for Adam. "I'll be there shortly. Anything else?"

Wyatt shot a look at Paige. "Does he need food?"

"I packed enough for a few days."

"Nope, think we're good," he told Adam.

"Give me the address you want me to meet you at."

Wyatt rattled it off. "Thanks, man. I'll owe you."

"No you don't," Adam said. "Not after the free labor

you donated to help get the boathouse in shape for the kids."

"I was glad to do it."

Adam had told him why the camp was so important. A hot lump of pain sat in Wyatt's chest as he thought about his friend losing a kid he was trying to rescue. Wyatt understood that kind of hurt, what it meant to lose someone you were supposed to watch out for. It wasn't something he wanted to experience again, which was curious considering he now had a woman who needed his protection sitting beside him in the truck.

This is different.

Yeah, it was different. They weren't in the high desert doing recon on a terrorist training camp. They weren't walking into an ambush that only a few of them would escape.

"So you don't owe me," Adam said. "Least I can do is help you with your puss— cat," he amended with a chuckle as Jane made scandalized noises in the background.

Wyatt rolled his eyes with a snort of his own. Some things never changed. He and Adam and the rest of the guys might not be teenagers in detention anymore, but there were times you'd never know it. One of the things he loved about his friends. No matter how much time passed, how far or how long someone stayed away from home, they were as tight as ever when they all got together again.

Which reminded him that he needed to call Jack at some point. It'd been too long since they'd spoken.

"See you in a bit," Wyatt said as he ended the call, still smiling to himself.

"Where was that address you told him?" Paige asked. "It's not my father's house."

"No, it's not. It's not safe for you to go there. If this guy could take a picture of you leaving your apartment building, he could also find you here. Your dad's place isn't a secret."

She made a noise of disapproval. "It has a state-of-the-art alarm system and cameras—not to mention a spa tub and an on-call chef."

Wyatt would have gaped at her if he wasn't driving. Was she seriously that shallow? A spa tub and a chef? "Yeah, and like I said—it's no secret. Once this guy knows you've left Seattle, it isn't too hard to get to Eagle's Ridge."

"But I could have gone anywhere! Europe, California, Hawaii. He won't know. What are the chances he'll come here?"

"Don't know… But are you willing to bet your life on it? What about your cat's life?" It was almost silly to consider a cat being under his protection, but the creature was as much his responsibility as she was. At least until he had to make a choice between them. In that case, it would be her every time. But for now the cat counted, if only because her stalker had threatened the animal.

Paige's tongue darted over her lips. Wyatt didn't like the way his groin tightened at that simple maneuver.

Whoa, was that a response? To *her*?

Maybe he'd imagined it. Paige Spencer was *definitely* not his type. She was too soft, too pampered. Too high maintenance. Beautiful, but she knew it. Shallow too.

"No, I'm not," she said softly, and the tension in his shoulders eased just a bit.

He really didn't want to argue with her anyway. As a SEAL, there'd been no arguing with those he rescued. They were grateful he and his team were there. But guarding a woman whose father was paying for his services was an entirely new experience.

"Good choice."

He turned onto another road and made his way up the side of the mountain, weaving through switchbacks as they climbed. Paige gripped the armrests. Once, her eyes were closed. Wyatt didn't say anything about it though.

Finally, he turned into the driveway he wanted and headed about a half mile off the road. A small cabin sat in a clearing at the edge of a cliff, the lights blazing. When the sun came up, the view of the valley and river would be spectacular.

He knew because he'd come up here earlier and checked it out. It was a newer build, a vacation rental, and though it was small and didn't have a chef, it was nice. Wyatt had stocked it with food and then set up a perimeter of cameras and equipment meant to let him know if anyone crossed into the zone.

He parked in front of the cabin. Paige blinked as she took it in.

"It's so small," she said.

Annoyance flashed through him. "Well, you aren't on vacation, are you, princess?"

Her head snapped around, her eyes widening. "You aren't like the other bodyguards I've had. None of them would talk to me like that."

"You mean I don't keep quiet and let you have your way?" Her lashes dropped over her eyes. *Guilty.* "I'll do my job, but I won't take orders from you. If anything, you'll take them from me."

"Nobody tells me what to do," she flashed back at him.

Wyatt opened his door and dropped a booted foot to the ground. "They do now," he told her. "Or you can get on the next plane back to Seattle."

Chapter 5

Paige steamed while Wyatt swaggered over to the cabin door and opened it. He really was an arrogant bastard. But he moved with such confidence and grace that she couldn't help watching the lines of his body.

"Stay there. I'll let you know when it's clear."

He inserted a key in the lock, produced a pistol she hadn't realized he was carrying, and disappeared inside. A few moments later he was back.

"You can come in."

Paige walked up the steps and inside the small A-frame cabin. She stopped and gaped at the tacky taste on display. Plaid furnishings, animal heads on the wall, a bear rug in front of a big stone fireplace that contained no fire.

Shame. It was June, but it was still cool enough for a fire.

The kitchen appliances were black, and the cabinets were some sort of blond wood that made Paige want to gag because *everything* in the cabin was the same tone. The walls, the cabinets, the floors.

She turned at the sound of Wyatt coming inside. He set down Mr. Fluffypants and then went back for her suitcases.

She hadn't needed to ask him, but she'd been prepared to do so. She was accustomed to the hired help behaving like they had jobs to protect, but this man was certainly different.

Not that she ordered people around or acted like a bitch. But when people were paid to do a job, she was a taskmaster. She'd learned that from her father. If you didn't ask people to do their best, they sometimes didn't do anything.

Wyatt returned with both her suitcases and pushed them across the floor. They rolled slowly toward her as he shut the door. She left them where they were and hurried over to crouch down by the cat carrier and pull the door open.

Mr. Fluffypants blinked at her with that superior mien of all cats and sashayed out of his confinement with his tail twitching and his nose in the air.

"How's Mama's baby?" she crooned. "Did he have a good trip? Would he like some yum-yums?"

He deigned to come over and rub his furry cheek against her fingers before strutting off to examine his new domain. Paige straightened, her eyes pricking with tears. *Safe.* When she'd read the letter from her deranged fan, she'd trembled with rage over the threats to Mr. Fluffypants. The threats to herself seemed surreal, but the instant her cat was brought in—well, that was the straw that broke the camel's back.

"That's a mighty big cat," Wyatt said, watching Mr. Fluffypants explore.

"He's a Maine Coon. They get big."

"Do they? I'm not a cat guy. Don't know much about them."

"Cats are misunderstood, but they're just as companionable as dogs. Maybe more so. They're very loyal."

Mr. Fluffypants chose that moment to walk over and sniff Wyatt's leg. Wyatt stared down at him and didn't move. Mr. Fluffypants strutted away as if he couldn't be bothered.

"I should get his food out." Paige went over and tipped a suitcase onto its side, unzipping it and taking out a box she'd packed. Thank God she had, really, since they hadn't stopped at a store on the way here.

She found a bowl in the cabinet and emptied a tin of food into it. Mr. Fluffypants came running over and sniffed it. Then he started to purr while he ate, though he didn't eat much before he was off exploring again.

"Poor bastard," Wyatt said, and she looked up sharply.

"What's that supposed to mean?"

"You called that poor thing Mr. Fluffypants—damn, I can hardly say it without feeling like an idiot. Why did you saddle him with such an unfortunate name?"

"I got him when he was a kitten. He was very fluffy and cuddly. The name just kind of stuck."

"Please tell me he has a real name. Like Spike or Bear or something."

"Mr. Fluffypants *is* his name. But I call him Fluffy most of the time." She wasn't about to say some of the other, more embarrassing things she called her cat. The Fluffmeister. Mr. Fluff-n-Stuff. Fluffernator. Fluffaluffagus.

"You want to be called something manly, don't you buddy?" Wyatt said as Mr. Fluffypants strolled by his leg and gave it a good rub on the way. The cat sat down and looked straight up at Wyatt. Then he meowed. "Yeah, thought so. Between you and me, I'll call you Spike."

Mr. Fluffypants meowed again. He rubbed Wyatt's leg for good measure and then strutted off. Paige hoped Wyatt's friend arrived with the litter box soon. She couldn't guarantee how the cat's bladder was holding up.

"You can take the master bedroom," Wyatt said, pointing to a hallway. "It's the only one on that end. I'll take the guest room."

Paige rolled her suitcases to the master, praying it wasn't covered in plaid comforters. It wasn't, but she didn't know if what was there was any better. This comforter featured forest camouflage complete with deer peeking out from the trees. Paige shuddered and tried to ignore it. Seriously, it was just fabric.

She opened her suitcases and found her toiletries, which she took to the bathroom. It was small but not offensive, with white tile and marble counters. She went back to the bedroom and dug through her clothing until she found something she could change into. Sweatpants and a sweatshirt with wool socks.

It felt good to slip out of the Louboutins. They were gorgeous shoes, but not all that comfortable for long periods of time. She turned on the shower, nearly groaning as she stepped under the hot water. It felt wonderful to scrub away the makeup and the dirt. After she was done, she dressed, twisted her hair on her head, grabbed her iPad, and went back to the living area.

Mr. Fluffypants was eating his food now, his explorations taking a back seat. Paige went over and flopped on the couch. Wyatt was nowhere to be seen. A minute later, the front door opened and he walked inside, carrying a load of wood in his arms. Her belly clenched at the sight of him. Wyatt William Chandler was shocking to the senses for some reason.

He was tall, broad, with dark hair and hot whiskey eyes. His face was easy to look at, which was seriously inconvenient. Paige hadn't had a boyfriend in months now, not since the last one turned out to be a douche. He'd been someone from her circle, which meant wealthy and refined.

He'd gone to Harvard, which he loved to tell everyone, and he was the vice president of his father's pharmaceutical company.

He was also a cheating bastard, which she'd discovered when he'd gone on a business trip and accidentally sent her a text message meant for someone else. So that had been the end of that.

She'd had a dry spell since, which was fine with her because she needed to concentrate on building her brand and getting her clothing line.

Right now, however, she was thinking that a nice slow ride on Wyatt's pogo stick might be just the thing to ease her anxiety.

Except he didn't seem to like her, so that was pretty much out.

Wyatt set the wood down beside the fireplace and started to stack a couple of logs in the firebox. "The litter box arrived while you were showering," he said, tipping his chin toward the kitchen. "Figured you could put it where you wanted."

"Thank you." Paige rose and went to retrieve the box and litter. She took it into the laundry room and set it up there with Mr. Fluffypants overseeing the operation. When she came out, Wyatt was in the kitchen and a fire blazed in the fireplace.

"You hungry?" he asked.

"Maybe. What do you have?"

He opened a cabinet. "I can offer you peanut butter and jelly, eggs, or a microwave meal."

"Peanut butter and jelly sounds good." She couldn't remember the last time she'd had that.

"I'm not fixing it. But I'll get the stuff out."

"I figured that. I can manage peanut butter and jelly."

Wyatt got out two knives and handed her one. Then he

set about fixing his own sandwich while she fixed hers. It was almost petty—but then she remembered that moment when she'd snapped her fingers at Bruce. She didn't like Bruce. He leered at her when he thought she wasn't paying attention.

So she'd been a bitch to him, and to Wyatt as well. It was no wonder he didn't want to lift a finger to do anything for her that he didn't have to do. Though he *had* carried all her luggage after all.

They made sandwiches in silence and then Paige retreated to the couch again, where she sat cross-legged, staring at the flickering firelight and the bear rug—and wondering what the poor bastard had done to get himself shot.

She felt a little like that bear, or how she imagined he must have felt. Trapped, cornered, backed against a wall.

She didn't like it. The sounds of scratching came from the laundry room. At least life was getting back to normal for Mr. Fluffypants. Her life was a different matter.

"Will I be allowed to go into town?" Not that she imagined they had much of anything to do in Eagle's Ridge. But it was better than staying cooped up the whole time.

Especially with a man who made parts of her tingle that she would rather did not. At least not right now when her life was so fraught.

"You can go, but not alone. I go where you go."

And didn't that thought make all her parts shiver?

"Is there anything to do in town?"

"Depends on what you want to do. There are shops. A library. A few places to eat and a bar."

"What kind of shopping?"

"Not the kind you're used to, I imagine. Boutiques, antiques, that kind of thing."

"Clothing?"

"There's a Walmart on the outskirts of town—did you forget something?"

"No. Just curious what you have here."

"There are knickknacks and stuff—touristy shops. I don't really know because I don't shop."

"I can see that."

He glanced down at his clothing—faded jeans that fit him far too well and had worn patches that highlighted parts she wished they didn't. He wore a gray flannel shirt over a black T-shirt, and his hair brushed his collar. On his feet were dark gray work boots that looked as if they'd been well broken in.

Not quite the type of bodyguard she was used to. The men she usually hired wore suits and faded into the background. She didn't think this man could ever fade into the background.

"I'm comfortable. And this isn't the red carpet," he said.

She had only to look at all the plaid surrounding her to prove that. "No, it certainly isn't."

"You might want to dress down while you're here. If you don't, you'll stand out like a sore thumb. You'll probably be uncomfortable too."

"I'll keep it in mind," she said. "So, how long have you been a bodyguard?"

"Counting today?"

"Well, yes."

One corner of his sensual mouth lifted in a grin that did things to her pulse. "Technically? About two hours now."

Chapter 6

Her pretty mouth fell open. She blinked at him. He could see the moment that her surprise turned to fear, and he berated himself for being an ass. She might annoy him, but she didn't deserve that.

"You're safe. Really." He dragged in a breath and shook his head. "I shouldn't have said it like that. This *is* my first bodyguard assignment. But I'm not new to security or combat. I'm a Navy SEAL. Or was."

Her body seemed to relax into the cushions again. So she knew what a Navy SEAL was. It would be impossible not to with all the TV shows and press about them.

She stared into the fire, and he could see the weariness lining her features. She'd washed away the makeup she'd been wearing earlier, but it didn't detract from her beauty. She was just as lovely without makeup as she was with.

"What happened?" she asked. "To make you leave, I mean."

That simple question slammed into his gut like a sucker punch. He didn't know why that was. He'd been asked by his friends why he'd left the Navy. Gran had asked. He'd given them answers, but not the right answer.

He wasn't going to give it to this woman either—but he wanted to. For once, he wanted to speak the words and let someone else know what a failure he'd been.

Except she wasn't the right person, was she? He was supposed to take care of her, not frighten her. And he *would* take care of her. He didn't want her questioning that.

"It was time to come home. My grandmother needed me."

"So you're from here?"

"Born and raised. My grandfather came shortly after the town was founded. He knew the founders when they were in the Army Air Corp together in World War II. Chandlers have been in Eagle's Ridge ever since."

"Isn't being a Navy SEAL dangerous? They're commandos who go after terrorists, right?"

"That's one of the things we do, yeah. And it can be dangerous. I've lost teammates before. Nearly been killed myself. That's part of why I came home—I'm all Gran has left."

"All she has left? Your parents are gone?"

"Rafting accident when I was three. Gran and Gramps raised me. He died a couple of years ago at age ninety."

"I guess it's good you came back then."

Wyatt didn't know why he was telling her these things. He got up and went into the kitchen, wishing like hell he could drink a beer but unwilling to do so while he was supposed to be guarding her. Instead he got a bottle of water and twisted off the top, downing half the contents.

She watched him from the living room, the firelight caressing her skin, highlighting the delicate structure of her nose and cheekbones. Her cat jumped up on the couch and nosed his way into her lap, flopping over like he'd run a marathon.

She dug her fingers into the silver fur and stroked him. He started to purr, the sound a steady rumbling that reached Wyatt where he stood. Paige bent her head and crooned soft words to him.

Wyatt suddenly wondered what it would be like to have those hands on his body. The stirring in his groin didn't surprise him this time. Apparently he was attracted to snooty blondes.

"Are you all right?" she asked, lifting her head to gaze at him. The cat blinked lazy blue eyes as if to say *You envy me right now, don't you?*

"Fine. You?"

"I think so. Just tired. It's been a long day."

"You should go to bed. Everything will be okay, I promise. I've got a security system, and I'm pretty good with a pistol." He was trying to be lighthearted with her, but the truth was he could kill with his bare hands if necessary. "Nobody's finding you here. Unless you tell them where you are. And I wouldn't, if I were you. You can't trust that the information will stay safe."

He'd made sure her phone's location was shut off earlier, but if she told someone where she was, it wouldn't matter.

"I won't tell anyone." She gently removed Mr. Fluffypants from her lap and stood. He looked incensed, but then he jumped down and ran to the bedroom where she was staying. Smart cat.

Lucky cat.

"Good night, Wyatt."

It was the first time she'd said his name. He liked the way it sounded on her lips. "Good night, Miss Spencer."

He was tempted to call her Paige, but he needed to stay

professional. Needed to keep that barrier between him and the client, no matter how pretty she was.

She smiled almost shyly before she hurried down the hallway and disappeared inside the master. She left the door open a couple of inches for the cat.

Wyatt found himself wishing he could sneak in there and lay his head in her lap while she stroked his hair like she had the cat's. He shook those thoughts from his mind and went over to open up the laptop he'd set up as his command center.

Time to check the cameras and see what was out there.

PAIGE WAS COLD. She blinked awake and stared up at an unfamiliar ceiling for half a second before bolting upright, her heart hammering. She scared Mr. Fluffypants, which made her squeal because she hadn't expected him to leap off the bed and streak out the door.

"I'm sorry, Fluffy," she called after him, her heart still pounding a mile a minute. But she remembered where she was as she took in the hideous deer comforter and wood walls of the cabin.

That didn't help with the cold, however. She threw back the covers and grabbed the sweatpants and shirt she'd discarded in favor of her pajamas last night. After changing—and realizing she'd failed to pack extra socks—she went over and pulled open the curtains on the french doors.

"Oh my," she breathed. She unlocked the doors and pulled one open so she could walk out on the deck. Her condo overlooked Puget Sound. She loved waking to that view.

But this one might be even better. It was early, and the

sun sparkled on green mountains crowned with white caps at their tips. There was a valley below, and what looked like a town far in the distance. The shimmery curve of a river snaked down the middle of the town. It wasn't a big town. Even from this distance she could tell there were no shopping malls.

The air was cool, and she wrapped her arms around herself. Her breath frosted and cold seeped into her feet from standing on the deck with no shoes. It occurred to her that if she'd gone to Hawaii, she'd have her toes in the sand instead of freezing them off.

But she hadn't wanted to be so far away, in case the studio decided to resume taping. It would take her only a handful of hours, including waiting at the airport, to make it back to Seattle. Hawaii would take a whole day.

She didn't think they were going to resume anytime soon, but she could hope. It wasn't about the money. It was about freedom and the ability to make her own way without taking orders from her father.

A thud sounded behind her. She whirled as Wyatt charged through the french doors.

So many things hit her senses at once. His hair stuck up as if he'd just gotten out of bed, and he had a weapon that he quickly dropped to his side when he stepped onto the deck. But holy hell, it was the fact he was only wearing a pair of athletic shorts that had her pulse zipping into outer space.

His chest was broad and packed with lean muscle. He had a tattoo on his left pectoral that she recognized as the Navy SEAL trident. Thank God for hot actors doing network series about SEALs these days, or she wouldn't know that's what it was. She was kinda glued to those shows. Probably a lot of women were.

This man was not a hot actor. He was the real deal. A

lethal commando who painted his face and parachuted behind enemy lines to rescue hostages or stop terrorists. Or used to anyway.

He was also hot. Incredibly hot. His pistol dangled at his side, and his shorts clung to his package. The outline was, er, large and prominent.

Paige shivered anew, but she didn't think the crisp air had a thing to do with it. Her nipples tightened. She prayed they weren't showing through the thick material of the sweatshirt, but with her luck they probably were. At least she could blame the cold.

"You okay?" Wyatt asked, his voice gravelly with sleep.

"Yes... Is something wrong? Did King send another message?"

He came over and put a hand on her shoulder. She hadn't thought she'd sounded panicky, but maybe she had. A current of heat flowed from his touch, dripped through her body. She didn't care to analyze where it landed or what it was currently doing to her lady parts.

"He didn't. You're safe here."

She could feel the heat emanating off him, smell the woodsy scent that clung to his skin. It was part pine, part woodsmoke—and part cold steel. He squeezed her shoulder again. Her gaze lifted to his in spite of some small sense of self-preservation that told her not to meet his eyes. Not to let their gazes tangle at such close range.

She did it anyway. And her insides melted.

"There's an alarm on the door," he continued. "When you opened it, the alarm triggered on my phone. I didn't know if someone was coming in, so I had to check. I'm sorry if I scared you."

She sucked in a breath. "I wouldn't have opened the door if I'd known."

"It's okay. I should have told you." He gave her a

lopsided grin that flipped her belly. "Told you I'm new at the civilian side of things. Didn't think you'd wake before me."

"I'm an early bird."

"So am I. But it's barely five a.m."

"Wow. Really?" She hadn't looked at the time before she'd stepped outside. No wonder her feet were cold. The sun hadn't had a chance to warm the deck yet.

"Yeah." He tucked the pistol away in his shorts, the grip sticking out of the top of his waistband—where did he find the room? Wasn't he worried about shooting something off?—and turned to gaze at the pretty scenery she'd been admiring before he interrupted her. He pulled in a lungful of air and reached up to scrub his hands through his messy hair.

Paige nearly choked on her own tongue. His sides rippled, his arms flexing in the morning light. You could bounce a quarter off those abdominals. Even his thighs and calves were tight with corded muscle.

He was beautiful, and her lungs refused to work as the synapses in her body went into overload.

She must have made a noise, because he turned back to her, a quizzical look on his face.

"What's the matter?"

Speak, Paige. You have to speak. "Uh…" *Focus on something. Anything.*

The pistol grip was still there, still sticking out of his waistband. She nodded toward it.

"Aren't you afraid of shooting off a part of your anatomy you might need?"

He glanced down. Then he laughed. "The gun's holstered. Trust me, it's fine."

"You have a holster in your pants?"

"And a weapon too." He shook his head. "Sorry,

42

couldn't resist. Yeah, I have a holster. It's a sticky holster. Not going anywhere, and neither is the gun."

"I've never had a bodyguard who seemed as…" She searched for the word. "…as relaxed as you. They wear their guns in shoulder holsters beneath their coats and look constipated most of the time." She waved a hand in his direction. "And you just stuffed a gun down your shorts."

"I'm going to guess that your former bodyguards didn't have my training."

"No, probably not." Because she'd never noticed that easy confidence Wyatt had in any of her prior bodyguards.

He turned back to the view. "God, I missed this."

She went up to the railing and leaned against it, looking over the valley like he was. They were surrounded on three sides by trees, but the deck jutted out just enough to give them this view.

"It's pretty. But there's so much space," she added with a shudder. "And no coffee shops."

"You prefer the city?"

"Yes. No bears. No wildcats. The only wild animals there are the single guys looking for love."

"Not the single women too?"

"Oh, I'm sure some of them as well. I just haven't noticed since I only date men."

"Are you dating one now?"

The question shocked her. And pleased her. Was it inappropriate? Maybe. But she didn't care.

"I'm not. Why?"

"Just looking for angles on your stalker. You dump anyone recently?"

Disappointment tasted bitter, didn't it? Of course he wasn't asking about her love life for personal reasons. Not that she was interested even if he was—

Oh hell, who was she kidding? After that gorgeous

display of muscle and manhood, she was *definitely* interested. What heterosexual woman wouldn't be?

"Not recently, no. The police already asked me that question."

He shrugged, never taking his eyes off the view. "I must have missed that in the case files." He straightened from where he'd been leaning on the railing and turned toward the house. "You want some coffee?"

She had to drag her gaze from his flat belly and the gun grip protruding from his waistband. "That would be nice, yes."

His smile could power entire cities based on the storm it set to trembling inside her.

"Great, so would I. I'm gonna shower while you fix a pot."

Chapter 7

"How's the client?" Hawk asked.

There were many things Wyatt could say to that question, but he decided to stick to the basics. He glanced at Paige's closed door and presumed she was getting dressed. When he'd left her to take a shower a little while ago, he hadn't really expected she'd fix the coffee. But she had. Shocked the hell out of him.

He took a sip, half wondering if she'd spiked it with something. Hot sauce, for example. She hadn't. He relaxed and swallowed the first mouthful.

"She's doing okay. Not happy to be here, but she hasn't been a pain in the ass yet."

A pain in other places, but not in the ass. Yeah, seeing her on the deck this morning, her nipples poking through her sweatshirt like twin beacons, had sparked a reaction in his groin. Her long blond hair had hung down her back, and her feet were bare. She'd looked sweet and sexy and anything but the high-maintenance heiress the dossier had painted her to be.

Yeah, she'd sparked a reaction all right. He'd been

fighting the mother of all erections while trying to be casual with her. It hadn't been easy. Or fun.

"That's good. Her father said she was strongheaded."

Wyatt was predisposed not to like her father, though he wasn't quite sure why. Maybe because of the way Paige had seemed so stunned when she'd realized he was taking over from Bruce. Nobody had told her that, and she'd been upset.

Made him think that maybe her father didn't discuss things with her, even when those things involved her.

"She's fine. A little put out to have her life turned upside down, but that's understandable."

"It is." Hawk sighed. "No news on this guy who calls himself King. No fingerprints on the envelope, paper, or photo. I've got a couple of detectives watching her apartment building for suspicious characters, but so far everyone checks out. The disgruntled studio employee turned out to be clear as well. No new suspects."

Wyatt and Hawk talked for a few more minutes before ending the call. Spike—because Wyatt refused to call the poor thing Mr. Fluffypants—came over and rubbed around his ankles for a few seconds. Wyatt reached down and scratched the cat's head. He was rewarded with a flop onto the side and a loud purr.

Paige emerged from her bedroom then. She looked hot in a pair of jeans with a tank top beneath a filmy shirt, and high-heeled boots that reached to her knees. She also looked expensive.

She took one look at Spike sprawled on the floor and grinned up at Wyatt. "He likes you."

"That's because I call him Spike."

She frowned, but he didn't think it was a real frown. "He doesn't know you're calling him that. Call him Fluffy. He'll respond to it."

"Fluffy isn't very masculine, is it, Spike?" he asked the cat. Blue eyes blinked up at him. Spike yawned, showing long white teeth.

"He doesn't have any balls. Masculine means nothing to him," Paige said.

"Damn, girl, you had his balls cut off?"

"He's happier without them, I assure you."

Wyatt snorted. "I bet he'd be pretty damn happy with them."

Paige shook her head. "Men."

Wyatt squatted down to pet the cat. "I don't know what she means by that, buddy, but I'm on your side. Us men have to stick together."

The cat basked in the attention, rolling to his back and exposing his belly. Wyatt started to reach for the silky fur when Paige made a *tsking* sound.

"I wouldn't. He'll claw you silly if you do."

Wyatt hesitated. "Really? He looks like he wants a belly rub."

"He doesn't, believe me."

Wyatt gazed at Spike. "And here I thought we were starting to like each other," he told the creature before getting to his feet. Spike flipped over and trotted to Paige, performing the same act on her legs. Traitor.

"How's Mama's Fluffy Boy? Has he been an angel?"

"If you call doing nothing except sleeping being an angel, then yeah, he's been an angel."

Paige cooed to the animal. "Oh, I knew Mama's boy was a good boy. Isn't that right?"

"Do you have Spike on the show with you?"

Paige looked up. "His name is Fluffy. Stop calling him Spike."

She was kind of cute when she was annoyed.

"Or what?"

She blinked—and then her jaw firmed in resolution. "I'll give you a bad review on whatever site people review bodyguards on. You'll never work again."

She stuck her nose in the air, but the trembling at the corners of her mouth said she wasn't serious.

"Bullshit."

"You're right, I won't type up a review. I'll just tell everyone who asks me for a bodyguard recommendation *not* to use you."

"I'm not worried."

"You should be. I've been asked precisely zero times for bodyguard recommendations. I could devastate your career."

He snorted. Why'd she have to be so cute? "Thought so." He nodded at the cat. "Is he on the show or what?"

She straightened. Fluffy—since she insisted on the name—jumped onto the back of the couch and settled down near where she stood. He kinda crushed the cushion though.

She ran a hand through his silky fur. "It's a reality show. The cameras follow me around—yes, he's been on when they've been in my apartment."

Wyatt shook his head. "Why would you let a group of people into your home to film your life? It's a pretty big invasion of privacy, isn't it?"

"It is. I had hoped it would take me places though."

"Take you places? You're already rich. What more could you want?"

She looked away, and he thought maybe he'd crossed a line somewhere.

"I'm sorry," he said. "Don't answer that." Because he understood that some things weren't meant to be discussed.

"No, it's okay." She leaned a hip against the back of

the couch while she petted Fluffy. "I want to be a brand. Like Paris Hilton. I want to call my own shots. And…"

"What?"

"I love clothes," she said, looking suddenly fierce.

As if she expected him to argue with her. He wouldn't dream of it though. Not right now when she seemed so passionate.

"I love seeing how clothes transform people. Especially women who lack confidence. I want to design a line of clothing that helps women put together stylish outfits that are also affordable. That's the problem, you see. Women walk into a store and they have no idea what goes with what or how to put it all together—or what sizes to choose since everything varies so much. If they're lucky, there's a good sales associate to help. If they aren't lucky, someone will ask them if they need help finding something and then walk away when they say no. Women don't know how to shop, and they get overwhelmed by choices."

Okay, so he had to admit he was a little speechless. He hadn't expected that to come out of her mouth. He hadn't expected she thought of anyone other than herself and her cat.

"So why not skip the show and go straight to the clothes designing?"

"I don't have that kind of money. My father has the money—and he's not going to bankroll a venture like this. I want to do it myself. I want to use my popularity from the show to seize on ventures of my own. No one will bankroll you when you're a nobody. When you have name recognition and a giant viewership? They want to cash in on it, so they'll sign on. I want to take advantage of that and build my empire."

She surprised him. Far from being the idle rich, this

woman had drive and big plans. He wouldn't have thought so just a few hours ago.

"I'm sure you're going to get what you want," he said. "It's just going to take time."

"I hope you're right." She didn't look convinced.

"You know what we say in the SEALs?"

She shook her head.

"*The only easy day was yesterday.* It's always a shit show, princess. Every day you pick yourself up and you do the best job you can. You keep on going because the alternative sucks. You fight for what you want. And you keep fighting until you get it."

"I don't intend to quit."

He grinned. "Then you're already halfway there."

Chapter 8

By midmorning, Paige was bored. She wasn't the kind of person to sit around doing nothing, so all this idleness was killing her. She tried reading a book. Tried watching television. She surfed the web, reading fashion blogs, and she did some sketches of ideas she had for a few outfits.

But it wasn't enough. She was accustomed to a frenetic pace in the city, especially with *American Princess*. She had meetings with her agent, meetings with the studio, and pitch meetings with fashion executives.

And when she wasn't doing all that, she was in front of the cameras, hanging out with the four other princesses and generally being as outrageous as she could be. She'd known going into it that she had to shine. She wasn't the prettiest one—that honor fell to Lily Ashwood, her best friend, but Lily was quiet and not likely to draw attention if she could help it. The other three women were varying degrees of whiny, catty, and bitchy.

But Paige could out-bitch them all. Audiences loved her for it too. Or had.

She tried not to think about what would happen if the

show didn't come back, but she wasn't very successful. If it didn't, she'd have to start over again.

She got up and paced the living room. Wyatt looked up from his computer but went back to whatever was on-screen. She had a crazy urge to go over and take his face in both hands, press her mouth to his, and see what happened.

Just to relieve the boredom.

Like that was the only reason.

Paige stalked out onto the deck and gripped the railing, rocking back and forth while gazing at the scenery. A bird circled high overhead, wheeling and drifting on currents. She envied that bird.

She turned and went back inside, closing the door and propping a hand on her hip. Wyatt looked up again. This time he arched an eyebrow.

"I'm bored," Paige said. "I want to do something."

Oh crap, had she really just said that? Because the moment she did, all she could think of was the very obvious thing that a man and woman alone together could do. It would certainly relieve her stress.

"There's a good reason to stay out of sight, Miss Spencer."

She hated when he called her Miss Spencer. Which was odd considering every bodyguard she'd ever had called her precisely that.

"Call me Paige. I insist."

"All right. Paige."

She liked the way he said her name. The shiver of anticipation it sent down her spine.

"I forgot to pack socks. Maybe we could go buy some?"

"I can have one of my guys bring socks here."

Paige felt like stomping her foot. She wouldn't though. That was the kind of thing she did on *American Princess.*

So bitchy.

"I'll wear a hat. And sunglasses. I'll put my hair inside the hat. No one will know I'm me. Assuming that's what you're worried about," she added.

"Not exactly. I'm sure some people out here watch your show, but the few I asked had never heard of it."

Paige blinked. Well, wasn't that just a kick in the pants? "So what's the problem then? Do you really think King will come here hours after I did? And that he'll find me? Eagle's Ridge can't be *that* small."

He was frowning. "The problem is we don't know anything about him. We don't know what he looks like or what he knows. It's safest to stay isolated until the threat is over."

"I think that's overkill, Wyatt. I think you just don't want to go anywhere."

He sighed and rubbed his forehead. "You're not going to stop, are you?"

Triumph was within her grasp. "Just a short trip. For socks. Please?"

He seemed to make up his mind about something. "All right. But you aren't Paige Spencer in town. You'll need another name."

"My middle name is Nicole. My mother's maiden name is Allen."

"Okay, Nicole Allen it is. Don't forget who you are or I'll be forced to drag you back here kicking and screaming. And don't think I won't. Nobody in Walmart would mind, especially if I said you were getting mouthy with me."

"Seriously? Isn't this the twenty-first century?"

He snorted, and she realized he was teasing her. "Just don't forget your name, Nicole. Or the fact you're my girl-friend from back in Virginia."

Paige's eyebrows climbed her forehead.

Wyatt spread his hands. "My best friends know who you are, but they won't tell anyone. Everybody else needs to think you're someone else. There's no reason for me to be hanging out with a strange woman in town unless I know her. And since I just moved back from the Virginia area a couple of months ago, it makes the most sense."

Paige grabbed her purse and shouldered it. "Did you leave a girlfriend back there?"

"Nope. But I can pretend. Can you?"

Paige swallowed at the heat in his gaze. "What are we talking about here? Some light PDA? Tongues? Public groping?"

"Let's start with the PDA and see how far we go."

Paige shivered. PDA with Wyatt? She could definitely do that. In fact, she looked forward to it. Probably more than she should. But it was exciting and distracting, and she could use both those things right now.

She checked Mr. Fluffypants's dishes, made sure they were filled with food and water, and then went to put her hair into a messy bun. She was wearing jeans and boots—without socks—and a tank top beneath a gauzy blouse. It was casual and cool, but she'd take a light jacket along in case the weather turned chilly. She slicked on lip gloss, double-checked her eyeliner, and headed for the living room.

Wyatt was waiting. He gave her the once-over but didn't say anything.

"Too much?" she asked. "Should I put on flip-flops?"

"You're fine."

He went over and opened the front door, waiting for her to walk through. She wondered as she passed him—as his heat and scent wrapped around her—where he'd put the pistol this time.

He locked the door behind them and hit the button to

unlock his truck. He even opened the door for her. She climbed inside with her heart beating just a little harder than it should.

"Will the house be okay?" she asked as he started the truck.

He looked at her with such confidence that she felt her nerves relaxing beneath her skin.

"It's fine. Spike is going to be okay by himself. Unless he figures out how to disarm the system. Doubt he will though."

"Fluffy," she said, and he laughed.

"I know. I just like yanking your chain, princess."

Oddly enough, she liked it too.

———

"WOW," Paige said as they drove down Main Street. "There are a lot of military monuments in this town."

They'd crossed the Sentinel Bridge with its statues of the four founders—two at each end—and now they were passing the World War II memorial. There was also a Korean memorial, a Vietnam memorial, and memorials to the most recent wars in Afghanistan and Iraq.

"Eagle's Ridge is a military town. Not in the standard way of being near a base and thriving on government contracts, but the town was founded by military men. There's a long tradition of military service here. Men and women from this town have fought in all our nation's wars since World War II."

"Is that why you joined up?"

"Yeah. It seemed like the thing to do. My granddad was thrilled with my decision—he was still alive then. Gran wasn't so much, but she didn't say anything."

"She didn't want you to go?"

"She wanted me to go to college and settle down."

"You said she lived here in town. Does she still live on her own?"

Wyatt snorted. "Oh yeah. Gran is only seventy-eight. Quite a bit younger than my grandpa was. She was recently diagnosed with diabetes, but that hasn't slowed her down. I thought I was coming back home to take care of her, but she's having none of it. She made me move into the apartment over the garage."

Gran said a young man needed his own space and living with his grandma wasn't going to get him laid, much less married. She'd actually said *laid*. He'd nearly fallen out on the floor. Whoever Gran was hanging out with these days, she'd gotten sassy as hell thanks to their influence.

Paige was grinning. "So you live in an apartment over your grandmother's garage?"

"For now." He took a left turn toward the town square and the shops there. "What about you? Who pays for your apartment?"

Her smile turned brittle and he wanted to kick himself.

"Daddy, of course. But I told you that earlier."

Wyatt flexed his hands on the wheel. "I'm sorry. I'm being an ass."

"It's okay. I'm used to it."

"You shouldn't be. And what I said wasn't directed at you." No, it was more like his own frustration at leaving the Navy and coming home to this.

Yeah, he'd done what he had to do—he'd left the Navy and come home so Gran didn't have to sit at his funeral and receive a folded flag delivered by an honor guard. But he still regretted his decision sometimes. And now he was taking it out on Paige Spencer.

"I sometimes think I quit the Navy for nothing. I'm here, but she doesn't need me. I want to take care of her, but she won't let it happen. She won't even let me go to her appointments with her. Makes me drop her off at the door and pick her up when it's done."

Paige reached over and squeezed his arm. It was a quick gesture, but his skin sizzled from the contact. Maybe hers did too since she dropped her hand so fast.

"Maybe it's not about you, Wyatt. She's a grown woman and she's used to taking care of herself. She's also growing older—maybe letting you go with her feels too much like losing her independence."

He pulled the truck into a free parking space in the town square and turned to her, one arm on the wheel, the other on the back of the seat. What she said made a lot of sense.

"I never thought of that."

She reached for his fingers where they dangled from the seat back. She didn't hold them, merely stroked the tips. He felt her touch all the way to his groin.

"I'm just guessing. But based on my own feelings, it sounds right. I had to fight my father to move out of his Mercer Island home. But when he married Melanie— Well, that was the last straw for me. Did you know that we went to the same college? She's my age. She met my dad when she came home with me on spring break once. She was my friend—and now she's my stepmother." She shook herself, and he felt a twinge of sorrow for her. "It's not fun when you feel as if you aren't in control of your life anymore. That's what your grandmother wants. Control. Doesn't mean she doesn't love you or want you here."

He could seriously kiss this woman. Hell, why didn't he? He dropped his gaze to her mouth. Her pretty pink mouth. She darted her tongue out, and he felt the twinge in his groin. The twinge he'd been feeling since the moment he'd picked her up at the airport.

Paige Spencer and all her hoity-toityness. Her hot-blonde snootiness. He wanted to kiss the daylights out of her. Then he wanted to strip those tight jeans down her thighs and bury himself between them. But not before licking her into a screaming orgasm. He had a feeling she would fly apart so sweetly.

"You're pretty smart for a city girl," he growled, curling his fingers around her slender neck.

He could feel the quickness of her pulse, see the beat of her heart throbbing in her throat.

"What are you doing?" she asked, her voice strained.

"Doing? This," he said, tugging her closer. Her mouth was right there. Right within his reach. He dropped his gaze to her plump lips. To their pretty pinkness.

"Wyatt," she breathed, her lashes dipping to shield her eyes, and he knew he had her.

He crossed the distance between them. And then he kissed her.

Chapter 9

Firecrackers exploded in her brain. Little bursts of light that rained down like a million fireflies buzzing around her head. Wyatt's lips on hers were light, teasing. He didn't take. He gave.

Paige wanted more. Her body responded with a flash of heat between her legs. She leaned into him, asking for more, her mouth opening beneath his.

He gave it to her, his tongue slipping inside her mouth to caress hers. Someone moaned and—

Oh hell, it was her. Her heart raced and her pulse thrummed and her body melted. She'd been kissed plenty of times, with varying levels of skill, but none had made her feel quite like she was going to come out of her skin at any second.

Wyatt cupped her face in his hands and made love to her mouth. He licked and sucked and teased, kissing her with a skill that made all coherent thought fly right out of her brain.

She wanted to touch him. Wanted to spread her hands on his bare chest. Lust was a powerful drumbeat in her brain. It had been so long since she'd felt a man's touch. So long since she'd wanted to. She'd been focused on success. Men didn't fit into that equation. Not yet anyway.

But this one—oh my, this one.

He kissed the daylights out of her, made her want things she'd forgotten in her quest for independence. It wasn't weakness to want to be held. Wasn't weakness to want someone to cherish you, even if only for a night.

Paige ran her fingers into his hair, curled them in the silky strands, and sucked on his tongue. He answered her with more intensity.

And then he broke away, sat back in his seat, and left her scrambling for her wits. She could only stare at him, at that sensual mouth, and wonder why he'd quit when it felt so good.

Her body zinged with sparks. Her feminine core ached with need. She was wet and hot and frustrated.

He shoved a hand through his hair and glanced out the window. "Shit."

Paige started to tell him where he could stick his regrets, but she caught someone moving out of the corner of her eye. A woman with silver hair, wearing a colorful caftan, bustled toward Wyatt's truck.

"Oh, for the love of God," Wyatt muttered as she kept on coming.

His window rolled down as the woman hurried up to them. Her gaze skated past Wyatt and bored through Paige. The woman's eyebrows rose and fell as if there was some sort of communication with an alien ship going on. Paige watched in fascination.

"Hello, Mrs. Fontana. What can I do for you?" Wyatt asked her.

"Nothing, Wyatt. Nothing at all. Hello, dear," she said,

still staring at Paige. "I'm Hildie Fontana. Owner of Hildie's House."

"Nicole Allen," Paige said, remembering to use the name they'd agreed upon. "I'm just visiting Wyatt for a few days."

"Hmm," Hildie said, her gaze darting between them. "I don't recall Wyatt mentioning any guests."

"Didn't know she was going to be able to make it," he interjected. "And I didn't want to jinx myself by telling everyone."

"Oh my, well." Hildie giggled as if she'd just learned a secret. "I can't believe Mary Beth didn't mention you had a girlfriend. But then she also didn't mention she had diabetes either. Gracious, that woman has gotten good at keeping secrets."

"Gran doesn't know about Nicole," Wyatt said, his voice smooth. "I didn't tell her because I thought it was over between us. We're trying to patch it up."

Hildie's eyebrows waggled more than ever. "It certainly looked like you were doing a good job of it to me."

"Hormones," Paige said. "You know how crazy they can be."

Hildie looked shocked, but then she laughed. "Oh my, yes. Crazy hormones run amuck. Well, I'll let you two get back to it. I've got work to do. Bring Nicole to the shop, Wyatt. You can show her those shelves you put up. Maybe browse the jewelry section. We have some lovely estate jewelry that just came in."

Wyatt's jaw was tight. "I'll do that, Mrs. Fontana. Thank you."

Hildie gave them a wave as she scurried away toward one of the shops on the square. Wyatt leaned his head back on the seat and closed his eyes.

"You look like you want to say a bunch of naughty words right about now," Paige said.

"Hell, yeah. And bang my head on the steering wheel a few times."

"Why? She seemed harmless enough."

"Harmless? You ever play the gossip game?"

"You mean the one where you tell someone a secret and then it gets passed around until the last person says it aloud and it's nowhere near the same as when you first said it?"

"That's the one. Hildie is the real-life equivalent. She lives for gossip. That woman has her nose in everyone's business. Always has."

"So you're telling me she's about to start calling everyone she knows and telling them she saw you kissing a woman in your truck?"

Paige shivered anew at the memory of that kiss. She wanted to do it again even if it was a bad idea. Which it probably was. Wyatt Chandler was a small-town boy and she was a big-city girl who was running back there the first chance she got. It was silly to start something that couldn't go anywhere.

"She'll have us engaged with a baby on the way by the end of it. Or maybe you're my secret wife come for a visit. With Hildie, you never know." He sighed and shook his head and turned the key.

The engine fired up and Paige frowned. "What about my socks?"

"They'll have to wait. I'll be about five minutes too late, but I need to get to Gran's and tell her what's going on before Hildie works her into a tizzy."

Paige didn't expect the tummy flip that happened at those words. She was going to meet his grandmother?

"Which version are you telling her?"

His whiskey eyes were somber. "The truth. I won't get Gran's hopes up by letting her think you're my girl. She'd love for me to get married and start having grandbabies. I won't let her think that's going to happen when it's not."

"You don't want to get married? Or have any kids?"

He shook his head. "Didn't say that. I'm not against it, but I haven't met anyone I'd want to spend my life with, much less take on the responsibility of raising tiny human beings with."

They passed onto the bridge with the two statues standing sentry at either end. The restaurant in the center was a rather interesting feature, but she didn't want to ask about it when he was talking about things like marriage and babies.

Though why she found that fascinating she couldn't say. It wasn't as if she'd had her heart set on either of those things. In her experience, marriage didn't last and babies were things you shuffled off to nannies and private schools. Neither was in her vocabulary.

"I think it's smart to be careful."

He shot her a glance. "What about you?"

They turned onto a tree-lined street with small Craftsman-style homes set on lush lots blooming with flowers. Sidewalks lined both sides of the street, and a few people were out in yards, pushing mowers or digging in gardens. It was cute. A real slice of small-town Americana.

Paige pictured a little cottage with Mr. Fluffypants in the window and a little boy running around the yard. Wyatt sat on the lawn mower, sweat dripping down his sexy torso, while Paige poured lemonade from a glass pitcher. A little girl with pigtails helped. Paige was wearing a skirt and high heels, and her hair was held back with a scarf.

Oh dear heaven…

She shook herself. He was still waiting for an answer.

"I've never really thought about it. I like kids well enough, I suppose, but I've never pictured myself with any."

He didn't say anything else as they turned into a driveway. The house was adorable, a Craftsman painted a light yellow with black shutters and a wide porch. There was a flowering vine that twined up the posts of the porch and over the entry, and a porch swing that sat empty.

Flowers bloomed in profusion in the garden, and the yard was a lush green. Behind the house sat a two-car garage with an apartment over it. Wyatt's apartment.

He killed the engine and swung from the truck. Paige followed. He gave her a look before they stepped up onto the porch. Frustration? Embarrassment? She didn't know. A cute little plaque on the mailbox beside the door said M.B. Chandler.

Wyatt knocked on the door. She would have found that odd, but then she thought maybe it wasn't wise to barge in on his grandmother. A few seconds later, the door burst open and a small, blond-haired woman stood there. Blond?

Mary Beth Chandler didn't look seventy-eight. If anything, she looked about fifty-eight. She wore jeans and a T-shirt that said NEVER UNDERESTIMATE AN OLD WOMAN WHO RIDES A HORSE.

Paige blinked. Really? At her age?

"Hildie tells me you're engaged to be married," Mary Beth said, folding her arms over her middle and giving her grandson a stern look.

"Gran, you know that's not true. I'd have told you."

She looked beyond Wyatt to where Paige was standing. "Damn shame. Such a pretty girl too." She opened the door. "Well, get inside, both of you. Tell me what's going on without Hildie's spies listening in."

Paige preceded Wyatt into a homey living room with a

pale couch with flowery pillows and two Queen Anne chairs. There were antique tables, a piano, and oil paintings on the walls. Flowers in vases sat on every available surface. Paige felt as if she could sink into the cushions and read a book.

Except that Mary Beth didn't look all that inviting at the moment. She folded her arms over her chest and glared at them both. "Sit."

Paige sank onto the couch. Wyatt sat next to her. They didn't touch or look at each other. The scents of lemon and lavender wafted through the air. And, wait a minute, were those cookies she smelled?

"Yes, I made cookies," Mary Beth said, staring straight at Paige.

Holy wow, the woman was psychic.

"You can have one when you two tell me the truth."

"You can't be eating cookies, Gran," Wyatt said, and Mary Beth glared daggers at him.

"I know that, child. Doesn't mean I can't bake them for friends."

"Like you didn't sample one to make sure it was good."

"One never killed a soul."

"You're diabetic," he growled.

She popped her fists on her hips. This grandmother didn't look all that frail or grandmotherly to Paige. Not at all what she'd pictured when Wyatt had been telling her about his seventy-eight-year-old grandma he wanted to take care of.

"I *know* that, Wyatt William Chandler. Stop telling me what I already know."

Wyatt looked militant.

"Now, who is this lovely young lady and why were you kissing her in front of Hildie's store?"

Wyatt leaned forward, elbows on knees, head in hands.

"It's nothing, Gran. Nicole is a client. Remember the job I said I was taking yesterday? The reason I'd be gone a few days? Nicole is the reason. I kissed her because I lost my head for a second."

Mary Beth's eyes turned to Paige. "And why did she kiss you back?"

Paige shrugged even though she felt like she was currently speared on a pin beneath a microscope. "He's a good kisser. I couldn't help myself."

"Really?" Mary Beth looked pleased. Or maybe it was amused. Paige wasn't certain. "Maybe you should try again sometime. But not in front of the whole town, of course. I expect by nightfall I'll be getting calls about where people can send the baby blankets and booties they'll be knitting."

Paige's mouth dropped open. Wyatt still hadn't lifted his head. He pulled in a deep breath and sat up slowly.

"You can't tell anyone she's a client, Gran. It's top secret stuff."

"I get that, young man. I'm not an idiot. Your grandfather was in the OSS. I know how to keep a secret."

"Gramps was OSS before he met you," Wyatt said. "He was out by the time the OSS became the CIA."

"Doesn't matter. I still understand the value of a secret. And I know how to practice good OpSec."

"Oh my God," Wyatt groaned. "You did not just say that."

Paige had no idea what they were talking about, but it was fascinating to watch the back-and-forth between Wyatt and his grandmother.

"That's operational security," Mary Beth said. "In case Wyatt doesn't explain it."

"Gran, please."

"Thank you," Paige said. "I was a little lost."

She liked this woman. Mary Beth had Wyatt flustered as hell. It was cute.

"Is your name really Nicole?"

"No. It's Paige. Paige Spencer." Because there was no way this woman would tell anyone her real name. Paige believed that down to her soul.

"That's lovely, Paige. Please call me Mary Beth. Would you like a cookie?"

"I would," Paige said. "More than anything."

Chapter 10

Wyatt followed them into the kitchen, more because he wanted to watch Gran than anything. She'd better not eat a damned cookie. Though if she did, he didn't know what he'd do. Short of grabbing it from her hand—which would earn him a swift kick in the behind—he wasn't going to be able to stop her.

She went over to the baking rack sitting on the counter and grabbed some cloth napkins from the drawer beneath. Then she handed Paige two cookies on a saucer.

"Thank you, Mary Beth," Paige said.

"You're welcome, child."

"Do you want a cookie, Wyatt?" Gran regarded him with an arched eyebrow.

"Yes, ma'am."

She repeated the napkin, saucer and cookie routine, handing him two cookies.

"Milk?"

"That would be lovely," Paige replied.

Wyatt wanted to tell her it was a trap, but the words

wouldn't come out when he had a mouthful of Gran's famous chocolate chip cookies.

"Sit, both of you."

They took a seat at the kitchen table while Gran poured milk into glasses. She carried it over and set it down. A moment later she was back with a plate that contained two cookies and a glass of milk.

"Gran," Wyatt began, and she held up a hand to silence him.

"Mine are sugar free, Wyatt. I bought them when I went to the store for more flour." She took a nibble of the cookie and sighed. "Not quite the same, that's for sure."

"Do you ride, Mary Beth?" Paige asked suddenly, nodding at Gran's shirt.

Wyatt didn't know if she was changing the subject to get him out of a bad situation or just asking questions, but he was grateful anyway.

"I do indeed," Gran said. "There's a dressage barn about five miles out of town. I go there. Do you ride?"

"I did," Paige said. "I had a hunter when I was a teenager."

"You should ride again. It does wonders for the soul. And the body," she added. "I started taking lessons again after many years away."

"And you didn't tell me you'd started," Wyatt grumbled.

Wyatt didn't like that Gran climbed up on horses at her age. But she refused to stop. When he'd learned she'd taken up riding again, he'd nearly blown a gasket. Her horse—because of course she'd bought one of the damned things—was so tall she needed a ladder and a grappling hook to get up on top of him.

Okay, not really. But she did have to stand on a riser, called a mounting block, and get on that way. Wyatt wasn't scared of much—he'd danced with death more times than he could remember—but seeing Gran on that giant beast, appropriately named Zeus, had nearly scared the hell out of him.

Fortunately, Zeus was gentle. He did whatever Gran asked of him and never tried to unseat her. Thank God.

"I don't owe you any explanations, young man," Gran said sternly. She smiled at Paige. "As I was saying, you should ride again."

"I'd like to," Paige said. "One day."

"How about tomorrow? You can go with me for my lesson."

Paige shot Wyatt a look. He shook his head slightly, hoping she took the hint.

"I don't know, Mary Beth. I kind of have to do what Wyatt tells me to do. He's responsible for my safety, after all."

Gran cut a stern look at him. Yeah, she was still annoyed about the cookie thing. And the horse thing. But dammit, he wasn't going to lose her to some senseless and preventable tragedy too.

"Is it that bad, Wyatt?" she asked.

It took him a few seconds to catch up. "Yeah, it is, Gran. Someone is sending Paige threats. He even threatened to hurt her cat."

Gran frowned. "You won't let that happen, will you?"

"No, I definitely won't."

"Don't you think the poor girl could use a distraction in the meantime? Riding would help take her mind off it."

"I don't have anything to ride in," Paige cut in. "But I appreciate the invitation."

Gran reached out and patted her hand. "It's okay, sweetie. You can come another time if you prefer."

Wyatt didn't think that was true, but he wasn't going to

mention it. Once the Seattle PD found King and put a stop to this, Paige was going back home. Neither Wyatt nor Gran would ever see her again.

He thought of that kiss earlier and disappointment speared into him. Not at the kiss, but at the idea of her leaving. He wasn't quite sure why he'd kissed her, except it had seemed like the right thing to do at the time. Little did he know that frigging Hildie Fontana would catch them at it and he'd be forced to come to Gran's for damage control.

But in those quiet, blissful moments when he'd been caught up in Paige's mouth, in the feel of her kiss, he'd wanted nothing more than to strip her slowly and take her to heights she'd never forget.

Not gonna happen, but he'd wanted it. He'd come to his senses and pushed her away—but not quick enough. Hildie had seen them and now she was playing her game of gossip. By the time it was through, Wyatt would be getting married and have a baby on the way. Gran wasn't wrong about that.

"You need anything from the store, Gran?"

Light blue eyes speared into him. They still had the power to make him tremble in his boots even if he was six foot three and a badass former SEAL.

"I'm fine, Wyatt."

"I know. Just asking since we have to go into town. Thought you might want me to pick something up for you. Milk, bread."

"I'm good. Thank you for asking."

"I don't know when I'll be back in the apartment. However long this assignment takes. But if you need the grass cut or anything, just call me."

Gran took a bite of her cookie. When she made a face,

Wyatt knew she wasn't kidding him that it was sugar free. She set it down and speared him with a look.

"I was cutting my own grass before you came back to town, young man. I can manage."

"Yes, ma'am, I know that. Just offering."

"You have a job to do, Wyatt. I won't be bothering you while you take care of Paige."

"Could I have the recipe for these cookies, Mary Beth?" Paige blurted. "They are absolutely delicious!"

"Why of course, dear. I'll write it out for you."

Wyatt didn't bother to point out that Gran had a computer and could email the recipe. Nope, not going there, especially when he'd just had his ass handed to him over something as simple as cutting her grass. In fact, he decided it was best to keep his mouth shut for the rest of the visit.

It was best, but probably not likely.

Chapter 11

It was almost hot in Eagle's Ridge at the end of June. Paige was wishing she hadn't worn boots. Flip-flops would have been more appropriate. But it had been cool on the mountain this morning, so she'd dressed accordingly. It would have definitely been cool in Seattle. In fact, she'd checked her weather app and found it was raining.

Of course it was.

But here it was sunny, even if clouds threatened to turn the day to rain. They'd drifted in a couple of hours ago, right about the time Paige and Wyatt had arrived at his grandmother's house.

She liked Mary Beth. The woman was smart, sharp, and unwilling to give an inch. She wasn't like any grandmother Paige had ever known. In her circles, a seventy-eight-year-old woman would have had enough plastic surgery to make her look like a wax-museum replica of herself.

Mary Beth didn't look a day over sixty, but none of it was due to surgery. It was probably due to the horse Wyatt didn't like. And maybe the fact she cut her own grass.

Whatever the reasons, Paige thought Mary Beth was cool.

After they'd eaten cookies and talked about horses and cooking, Wyatt said it was time to go. Mary Beth had packed up a dozen cookies to go with them, and they'd walked out into the afternoon heat and climbed into the truck. He'd asked Mary Beth to go to lunch with them, but she'd refused.

"I'm hosting a canasta game at three. I have to get ready."

They'd said goodbye, and now they were making their way back through the neighborhoods of Eagle's Ridge. It was a cute town, but not the kind of place Paige could ever live. It wasn't vibrant. There were no clubs, no coffee shops —well, one coffee shop—and no designer boutiques. To live with that day in and day out? She had no idea how people did it.

Not to mention, the restaurant situation was dire. So dire that Wyatt pulled into a parking lot on the bridge and turned the key. "No Man's Land is the best diner in town," he told her. "We can get a bite to eat and then get your socks."

"Sounds great."

Paige gaped at the worn old building and figured there were no little cafes with three-Michelin-starred chefs hanging about. Probably no tablecloths or wineglasses in this place either. Not that those things made the food taste better, but they definitely made for a relaxing dining experience.

"Wyatt, how you doing, sweetie?" an older woman asked as they walked inside.

"Hi, Brenda," Wyatt said, returning the hug she gave him.

Brenda gave Paige the once-over. It was a friendly perusal. "Been hiding your girlfriend from us, Wyatt?"

Clearly, Hildie Fontana had been burning up the lines of communication in Eagle's Ridge for the past couple of hours.

"This is Nicole," Wyatt said. "We're talking about renewing our relationship. No guarantees."

"Hi," Paige said, shaking Brenda's hand.

"Well, darlin', you sure are a pretty thing. You two come on over here and have a seat by the window."

She led them to a booth that looked out on the river. It was a lovely view, even if there were no tablecloths. Brenda handed them two plastic menus.

"Do you know what you'd like to drink?"

Paige smiled. "What kind of white wine do you have?"

Brenda shook her head. "Oh honey, no alcohol in No Man's Land. Never has been."

Paige glanced at Wyatt for an explanation. No wine? Was this town dry or something?

"Eagle's Ridge was founded by four men. Two of them had a falling out and stopped speaking to each other. They lived on opposite sides of the river, so this spot became a sort of DMZ—demilitarized zone—where no arguments were allowed. It's much easier to prevent arguments when there's no alcohol. So there isn't, and never will be. Right, Brenda?"

"That's about the size of it. Though the Westbrooks and Tuckers have made up now, haven't they?"

Wyatt nodded. "Yep." He turned to Paige. "Ryder Westbrook and Bailey Tucker fell in love about three months ago. The feud is officially at an end."

"Wow. Only took, what, fifty-some-odd years?"

"More like sixty-five," Brenda said. "Been going on for a long time."

"Well, I guess I'll have water with a lemon," Paige said, deciding that asking for sparkling water was probably not a good idea.

"Water," Wyatt said.

Brenda walked away and Paige studied the menu.

"Confused?" Wyatt asked.

"A little. HALO pancakes drowned in rocket fuel?"

"Just pancakes and syrup. You in the mood for breakfast or lunch?"

"Lunch."

"If you like hamburgers, give the Bunker Buster a try. Bailey Tucker is a chef and she came up with a variation on the usual. There's smoked cheddar, avocado, and garlic aioli on that one. It's really good."

"Bunker Buster? Sounds terrifying."

Wyatt snorted. "Sam—that's Bailey's dad—insists on the military names. It's just part of the tradition."

"This town is… surprising," she said. "I feel like I'm in a military museum."

"Not your style, huh?"

Paige lowered her gaze, studying the menu again. "I appreciate the military and what they do. But I don't understand all the terms. I feel a little lost, if I'm honest."

"Eagle's Ridge is a popular tourist attraction. Partly because of our military traditions, and partly because we have great outdoor activities. It's high season at A To Z Watersports. My friends Adam and Zane can barely keep up with demand. We also have a huge celebration coming up for the July Fourth weekend. There's a parade, a carnival, and a fireworks display. Not quite worthy of Washington DC—but damn close."

Paige felt an unfamiliar twang strum against her heart. It took her a moment to realize it was envy. It wasn't that she suddenly liked small towns or wanted to uproot her life and quote—find herself—unquote in the pristine beauty of Eagle's Ridge. No, the envy had to do with belonging. Wyatt belonged here. No matter where he went in life, what he did, this place was waiting for him.

She didn't have that. She had a father who'd married a much younger woman and started acting like an idiot and a mother who'd moved to Europe with her artist boyfriend. Paige didn't have that sensation of belonging anywhere. She'd been raised all over, though Seattle probably had the biggest claim on her affection.

But even then, she didn't have the kind of connection there that Wyatt had here. In fact, since King had started messaging her, she'd felt more disconnected than ever. She'd realized that, aside from Lily Ashwood, she really didn't have any friends to speak of. Oh, she had people she could call, people who pretended to be besties with her, but that was the money talking, not a true sense of connection and affection.

The moment she couldn't do something for them, they melted away like snowflakes in the rain.

She set the menu down with a sigh. "It's too bad you don't have any upscale dining for the tourists."

"You don't like it here?" He looked perplexed. She didn't bother to point out the military decor and the lack of tablecloths—or wine, for heaven's sake.

"I'm sure the food is great," she began. "But sometimes a girl wants baby lettuce with heirloom tomatoes, house-made buttermilk ranch dressing, and deconstructed avocado toast."

"I'm not going to ask about that last one," Wyatt said with a frown. "But they've got salad here. And Brenda makes her own dressing."

"Would that be the Fields of France salad and the *Eisenhouser* dressing?"

Wyatt snorted. "Yeah, that's it."

Brenda returned then and Paige ordered the salad with toast and avocado slices on the side. She'd construct her own avocado toast. Wyatt ordered the Bunker Buster.

"We do have an upscale restaurant, by the way," he said once Brenda was gone. "Bailey opened Blue Moon at the beginning of May. It's been packed since."

Paige stared at him over the giant plastic cup of water. "And you brought me here?"

He glanced out the window at the admittedly gorgeous scenery. "You got a problem with No Man's Land?"

"No, but a glass of wine might be nice. And a tablecloth."

"Those two things add more than fifty percent to the bill."

"Yes, but I'm paying, so what does it matter?"

He lifted an eyebrow. "Thought it was going on my expense account."

"For which you get reimbursed."

He nodded. "True. But I don't want to make a bad impression on my first assignment."

"I'm sure it's expected when I'm your client, don't you think?"

"Maybe. Doesn't mean I intend to live like..." He didn't finish the sentence, picking up the fork and knife folded in a paper napkin instead. He broke the seal and smoothed out the napkin with the silverware cradled inside.

"Like a king?" she finished for him.

"Poor choice of words."

She shrugged. "It's okay. It's a ridiculous made-up

name. I refuse to be intimidated by it. So he thinks he's my king? No, I don't accept that."

Her words were brave, but whoever this guy was, he *had* rattled her. The photo proved he knew where to find her. He wasn't just a random crank who watched the show. He'd sent her vague threats in the past that had unnerved her—but the photo, and bringing her cat into it, took the threats to a whole new level of crazy. She was definitely intimidated. She didn't plan to admit it though.

"Thanks for changing the subject back there, by the way," Wyatt said.

It took Paige a minute to realize what he was talking about. "The cookie recipe? You're welcome."

"I was in big trouble there. You saved me."

Paige couldn't help but smile. "Your grandmother is a fascinating woman."

"She's stubborn."

"And you aren't?"

He turned his head for a second, gazing at the river rushing by below. "Maybe I am."

"Maybe so."

He met her gaze again. "I'm sorry about Hildie. I shouldn't have kissed you."

She tried not to feel disappointment. He wasn't saying kissing her was bad. Just that he shouldn't have done so. Well, maybe he shouldn't have. Maybe she shouldn't have kissed him back.

Too late. That cat was out of the bag.

"I liked it," she said, dropping her gaze at the last moment because she couldn't seem to look at him and admit it at the same time.

"So did I."

Her heart soared.

"But it can't happen again," he continued, and her

spirits deflated like a punctured balloon. "I have to protect you. I can't let it get personal between us. Mistakes happen when it gets personal, and I won't take that chance."

"It's okay, I understand."

But she didn't. Not at all.

Chapter 12

Wyatt ended up taking Paige to Walmart for her socks. Big mistake, because she got fascinated with all the stuff available in the store. At first it was cute, but then he ended up downright amazed at how unfamiliar with the retailer she was.

She'd walked up and down the aisles, picking up one thing after another, either marveling over the price or making a comment about the usefulness of the item. The woman had literally never been in a Walmart in her life.

Or, if she had, the experience was so long ago that she didn't remember a thing about it. In the end, she bought socks, a metric ton of toys for Fluffy, DVDs, junk food, and a box of wine. Yep, in Washington State, land of good wine, the woman who could afford anything she wanted bought a box of wine.

"It's good wine," she'd said defensively when he'd given her what must have been a disbelieving look.

He'd held up both hands and said, "I believe you."

He'd had his fill today of women who gave him hell for the slightest implication that she was wrong about something. Gran had ripped into him about cookies and lawn mowing. He'd learned his lesson.

They headed back up the mountain. It was late in the day by the time they reached the cabin. Wyatt carried Paige's stuff inside. By the time he set her bags on the counter, he remembered that he'd planned to make her ask him for help instead of automatically doing stuff for her.

Well, hell. He'd screwed that one up.

She was holding that damned cat, cooing to it, except the whole thing was ridiculous because the cat was huge and Paige wasn't.

Wyatt went over to his computer and booted it up so he could check the perimeter electronically. He'd seen no signs of incursion when they'd returned, but it was habit to check everything anyway.

There was nothing. A check of the visuals revealed some squirrels, a few deer, and a bear.

Paige had disappeared into her room with Fluffy. Wyatt headed for the bathroom near the guest room. He stopped hard in the hallway as the scent of something foul wafted to him.

He'd passed the laundry room, where the litter box resided, but this smell seemed to be coming at him from a different direction. He followed it down the hall. Into his room.

And there, in the middle of the bed, was a pile of what could only be crap.

He stared, blinking, for almost a full minute. *That feline bastard.*

Wyatt strode back down the hall, all the way to Paige's room, and thought about pounding on the door. But that might scare her, so instead he settled for a knock, though he was seething inside.

Damned cat.

"Paige, open up. I need to talk to you."

The door flew open and she stood there with wide eyes. Her feline companion lay in the middle of the bed, stretched out, tail flicking, blue eyes giving Wyatt the once-over as if to say *Oh yeah, puny human?*

"What? Is something wrong?"

"No. I mean yes. But nothing big." He swore internally. "Actually, it is big. Huge. A pile of shit in the middle of my bed."

Paige's eyelashes fluttered as if she were trying to comprehend. And then her mouth dropped open for a split second before closing, her jaw hardening. She spun.

"Fluffy, what did you do?"

He licked his paw, completely unconcerned. Paige whirled around again.

"I am so sorry. He never does that. I mean, not since I tried to have a roommate for a while. Mr. Fluffypants didn't like her and…" She swallowed. "Anyway, when she moved out, his incursions stopped."

Wyatt would have laughed if he weren't so pissed. Incursions? The damned cat was an operator, moving silently into his enemy's stronghold and wreaking havoc before the enemy knew what was happening.

And all the while, he lay on Paige's bed, staring at Wyatt as if he'd gotten the upper hand.

"I'm not moving out."

"No, of course not." She bit her lower lip between her teeth and he had a strong urge to suck that lip into his mouth. His groin began to ache at the thought.

No. Not appropriate. She's a client.

"I'm so sorry," she said, pretty hazel eyes wide and innocent. "If you want to go back to Walmart and buy a new comforter, I'm happy to pay."

"I am *not* going back to Walmart tonight," he growled.

"You're going to clean up your cat's mess and wash the comforter."

She drew herself up in her hoity-toity pose. "I'd really rather pay for a new one. Just throw it out, Wyatt. It's no big deal. They had so many to choose from, and they weren't expensive at all."

He reached up and gripped the doorframe, giving her a casual look. Was he holding himself back from wringing the cat's neck? Or showing his biceps to their best advantage even though he was pissed? And if he was showing off, what the hell did that say?

"Princess, you may be accustomed to throwing perfectly good stuff away because your daddy has more money than God, but around here we know the value of a dollar. There are people who'll spend tonight under a bridge, who'd love that comforter, cat shit and all, and you say toss it and buy another one? No. Hell no. Your cat did this, you fix it. And use that money to buy someone a blanket who really needs it."

Her cheeks were red. She tilted her perky nose up and he thought they were going to do battle right then and there. But she stepped out of the room and shut the door behind her.

"Fine."

She marched past him, into the kitchen, and grabbed a roll of paper towels. Then she went into the guest room. He followed, of course. She stopped short and stared.

"Oh my."

"Yeah, *oh my* is right."

"What did you do to him?"

"Do? Nothing. I got him a litter box, didn't I?"

Paige turned. "You did, but you also insisted on calling him Spike. I told you he didn't like it."

Seriously, was she crazy cakes or what? "He's a cat! He doesn't know the difference."

Paige smirked as she unwound a wad of paper towels. "Oh really? Tell me why else he did it. Did you swat him or something? Yell at him? Take away food?"

"No, none of those things."

"But you did call him Spike instead of Mr. Fluffypants."

"It's a ridiculous name."

"I told you to call him Fluffy. You didn't listen. You have also been rude to me. He senses it."

"Rude? Because I make you do your own chores and clean up after your cat?"

She huffed as she advanced on the pile with her wad of paper towels. A moment later, it was gone. The brown stain in the center of the comforter was not.

"If you had that hideous camouflage comforter from my room, you'd have never known this was here."

"Then I'm glad I don't have it."

She carried the crap into the kitchen and dropped it in the trash. Then she washed her hands.

"All you have to do is stick it in the washer now," she said, sniffing.

"No, that's *your* job," he told her.

"My job? Why? I cleaned up the mess."

"You didn't. You removed the most prominent evidence of the incursion. Cleaning up the mess means putting it back the way it was before the incursion happened."

She shook her head. "What the hell are you talking about?"

"Hey, you used the word first. Not me. But if you want to treat this like that little bastard is a commando, then trust me, from a commando's point of view, the mission is not complete. You have to remove all evidence and return the quarters to the way they were."

Paige blew out a breath. "You're nuts, Wyatt."

He was nuts? "I'm not the one with a twenty-pound male cat named Mr. Fluffypants."

"You really want me to wash your comforter?"

"And the sheets as well. Yeah, I do."

She blew out a frustrated breath and threw her hands in the air. "Fine."

Paige marched down the hallway to the guest room. He followed. She ripped the comforter and sheets from the bed, struggling to get the fitted sheet off. He almost went to help her, but she tugged it free at the last second and jerked the whole thing from the bed.

Then she carried the pile, though she could barely see over it, to the laundry room where she stuffed it into the washer. After a mumbling search for detergent, she found it and upended some into the washer. Then she closed the lid and twisted some dials before pressing a button. The washer started up with a smooth whirr.

"There. Satisfied?" She faced him with arms folded across her body, chin thrust out militantly. "You thought I wouldn't know how to do it, right? You wanted to test me? See if I knew the washer from the dryer?"

Wyatt stood in the doorway, arms folded over his chest, ankles crossed, watching her. "Something like that," he drawled as desire and admiration and anger all twined together in his gut.

He wanted to kiss her and he wanted to strip her naked and take her right here in the laundry room. On top of the washer. During the spin cycle.

Stop. Not happening. Down, boy.

Her nostrils flared and her cheeks stayed red. "Well, I

do know how. You don't think I have elves come in and do my laundry, do you?"

"No, but I bet you have a housekeeper."

Her nostrils flared again. "I do, and she does laundry. But she only comes a couple of times a week, and sometimes I need something sooner. So I learned how to wash my own clothes when necessary."

"Bravo," he drawled. Yeah, he was still pissed at the cat, still pissed at Gran and Hildie and even the fact he was in this situation instead of busting into an enemy enclave and kicking some terrorist ass.

No, he was busy babysitting a spoiled woman and her pampered feline. This is what his life had come to.

"You don't have to be so damned smug and superior," she growled.

"I'm superior? Me?" Who the hell was she kidding? "Princess, you've never been inside a Walmart in your life until today. And somehow I'm the superior one?"

Her face reddened. "I've been to Walmart, you rude bastard. It's been a few years, okay? I *liked* it."

Her eyes flashed hot. He wanted nothing more than to kiss her again. Nothing more. It might even be worth the dent to his integrity if he did.

Fury whipped through him.

"You're like one of those disaster tourists. Someone who visits those who are less fortunate than they are and then insist on using that visit to show how worldly and in touch they can be. While you go back to your safe bed at night, to your baby lettuces and avocado toast, those people are still in danger. Still struggling. But you'll write a check and make yourself feel better. Tell yourself you're doing an awesome job being a great humanitarian."

Her eyes were wide, wounded. He knew he should

stop. But he couldn't. Something bigger than him was taking over.

"In the meantime, those people who are marginalized will do desperate things. Some of them will radicalize, and then one day they'll be trying to survive, trying to gain an inch of ground in the misery in which they exist. They'll fight to the death, and they'll take down your buddies as they do. You'll kill them without mercy, because that's what you've been trained to do, but you won't forget. You won't damned well forget, especially when you have to face your buddy's wife and baby daughter and tell them how sorry you are for their loss."

He was breathing hard. Staring at her. Fists clenched at his sides. Her lip trembled. And then she lifted her arm, reached out her hand. Dropped it again.

"I'm so sorry, Wyatt. I had no idea."

Chapter 13

Tears clogged her throat. Tears of anger and shame for herself, and tears of sorrow for him. He blinked at her as if he'd been transported from another world and only now realized where he was. What he'd said.

He turned on his heel without a word and stalked out of the laundry room. She stood there for a full minute, reeling. He'd just told her something. Something that hurt him more than he wanted to admit.

If she'd understood correctly, he'd lost someone. And it had affected him deeply.

She stumbled out of the laundry room behind him, swiping angrily at her tears. What the heck was she crying for? Because he'd insulted her? Equated her with disaster tourists who went to impoverished areas and took selfies while helping the locals?

She wasn't that person. Though, yes, she wrote checks to the causes she believed in. She had money, had a trust fund, though she only received a stipend and not enough to wager it on her business ideas. If she had full access, she'd have her clothing line.

She did not.

And, right now, it didn't much matter. Wyatt was on the deck, leaning against the railing, staring at the town of Eagle's Ridge below. Or maybe he was looking at the mountains ringed in clouds. She didn't know, and she also didn't know what to say.

"I'm sorry," he said, his voice a deep rumble that rolled over her.

She joined him at the rail. Not too close. She propped her arms on the top rail and drew in a deep breath of clean mountain air.

"No, it's okay."

"It's not," he said, turning his head to capture her eyes with his. "I said some things I shouldn't have."

"You were mad. I understand. Fluffy was a jerk, and I guess I didn't take it seriously enough."

His comment about someone under a bridge being happy with a blanket with cat crap on it still stung. He was right, of course. She knew she was privileged. She tried not to forget it, but sometimes she clearly did.

"He's a cat. It's not like he had an elaborate plan. I overreacted."

She frowned. Maybe he did. Or maybe he was right and she was too spoiled to even know how good she had it. Did she forget about those less fortunate? No doubt she did. Because she didn't have to deal with them. She was so focused on her own life and success that she didn't think about it.

"No, you were right to call me out. I shouldn't have suggested you throw the comforter away. It was insensitive of me."

"The world's problems are not your fault, Paige. And you have enough to deal with right now."

"Thank you. But I'm not a disaster tourist, Wyatt. I

never have been. Yes, I send money to the things I believe in—women's rights and health worldwide, advocacy for the poor, feeding poverty-stricken nations, fighting against human trafficking. I'm not silent, though I am also not affected by those things. I know I'm fortunate."

She drew in a breath. "But you said something else… You said you had to face your friend's wife and daughter and tell them you were sorry for their loss. That sounds like you lost your friend. Was it on a mission?"

He dropped his forehead into his hands. Ran his fingers through his hair. Turned his gorgeous face to hers. His eyes were stark. "It's nothing. Forget I said it."

"I don't think I can do that."

"It's really easy, Paige. Think that you don't really know me, that we aren't friends or lovers, and that once this is over, you won't ever see me again. Think that you're the client and I'm the bodyguard. I'm an employee, not a friend. I'm here to protect you, not sit around the fire and talk about life. We don't mean anything to each other and we never will. So go back inside, pet your cat, and think about your future making clothing for women. Stop thinking about anything I said, okay?"

Her throat felt lined with razor blades. He wasn't going to tell her anything. Why did it hurt so much? Why did she care? She hardly knew him. "Okay. If you insist."

"I do."

She sucked in a breath, trying to tamp down the pain that insisted on throbbing inside her belly, her veins. She shouldn't be hurt by his unwillingness to share with her. She shouldn't care.

But she did. Damn him and his kiss today. Damn him for taking her to meet Mary Beth, whom she'd liked *so much*. No Man's Land wasn't anything special, at least not to her, but even that was going to be a memory she couldn't erase.

"I guess I'll go inside then. Thanks for the lovely day."

He didn't say anything as she spun and walked away.

HE WAS AN ASS. A dick. A total jerk. But what could he say to her? He'd lost his mind back there for a moment, and he'd let her have it. But it hadn't really been about her. It had been about the frustration and hurt building up inside him. The pain. The secrets. The things he wasn't willing to tell anyone.

Lisa, holding little Emma and thanking him for coming to Danny's funeral. Thanking him with tears in her voice. Telling him—my God, telling him that it wasn't his fault.

But he knew it was. It *was*. He'd failed to realize the threat. Failed to protect his buddy. And Lisa and Emma suffered as a result. Danny's parents, his siblings. They all suffered because Wyatt hadn't seen it coming that day.

He scrubbed his hands through his hair. Took a deep breath. Told himself that was over and done with. Lisa didn't blame him even if he blamed himself.

There was no reason to keep living with this guilt, and yet he couldn't stop.

He spun and went inside, shutting the glass doors behind him. The washing machine was still chugging away. The house was silent except for that. Still. Like that day on the mountain before all hell broke loose.

Holy shit, he was losing it.

He went over to the computer and sat down, going through the data. He had to concentrate on what was happening to Paige. Had to figure out who was after her and what kind of a threat the guy really was. Yeah, he'd threatened to hurt the cat. He'd also threatened to punish Paige if she didn't keep herself pure for him. Whoever he was, he was a sick bastard with a fixation.

And Wyatt had no idea who he was or what his next move would be. After an hour of studying everything, he had to give up on the idea. He shoved away from the computer and put his hands on his head, taking deep breaths and staring at the sunset happening just outside the window.

The washer had dinged long ago. He got up and went to the laundry room, tugging the tangled bedding from the washer and shoving it into the dryer. He turned it on, then headed for the kitchen. Paige still hadn't emerged from her bedroom. Neither had her cat. He was still pissed about the cat crapping on his bed, but in the scheme of things it wasn't that awful. It could be dealt with.

He took out a frozen pizza and turned the oven on to heat. Then he dialed Adam's number.

"Hey, Wyatt," his friend said, his voice happy and sane. Where was Wyatt's happy and sane? He couldn't seem to find it anymore. "Heard congratulations are in order."

Wyatt frowned for a sec. Oh yeah. "What's the story now? Marriage or a baby? Or both?"

"Well, I heard it was marriage. Jane heard your girl-friend from Virginia is pregnant and you're doing the right thing by her. I'm assuming Nicole is Paige—either that or you've *really* got your hands full."

Wyatt wanted to strangle Hildie Fontana right about now. But what had he expected, parking in the town square and kissing Paige in front of God and everyone? Hildie didn't mean to be a pain in the ass. She just was. But her husband and son had both died in service to this country, so if gossiping made her happy, then whatever. Wyatt could deal with the fallout. He didn't like it, but he'd deal.

"Yeah, Nicole is Paige. She wanted to get out so I took her to town. I kissed her and Hildie saw."

"Whoa, you kissed her? Haven't you known her for what, all of sixteen hours or so?"

"Pretty much. What can I say? She's hot."

Besides, Adam didn't have much room to talk. He'd ended up with the woman he'd hired to help him design the boathouse makeover. Wyatt didn't know how long before Adam made his first move on her, but he didn't think it had taken very long at all.

"Is it a good idea, Wyatt? I mean you're supposed to be protecting her, right?"

"No, it's not a good idea. It won't happen again. It was just—she said something about Gran that made sense to me. Made me think about some things. I was a little too grateful."

"I get it. I think. So what's up? Need more cat litter?" Adam laughed and Wyatt shook his head.

"No, we've got enough…" Especially when the little bastard wasn't using the box. "Hey, I wanted to ask you something."

This is where his throat closed up and his eyes stung. *Dammit.*

"Anything, Wyatt. You know that." Adam must have sensed that it was serious.

Wyatt stood there for a long minute, staring at the mountains as they turned golden in the early evening sun. It was so beautiful. So peaceful.

So why wasn't he at peace?

"When does it stop eating you up inside?"

Adam sighed. "I don't think it does. I think you learn to accept it and go on with life. It's all you can do… You want to talk about it, man? About what happened?"

"No."

"All right. But I'm here when you do. All of us are."

"I know." He pulled in a breath. "Hey, thanks. I gotta run. Have to heat up a frozen pizza for the princess."

The amusement returned to Adam's voice. "Good luck with that."

"Yeah. I think I'm gonna need it."

Chapter 14

Paige smelled something cooking. She sat up in bed and sniffed the air. What was he making? And was he making enough for two, or when she walked out there, would he tell her she was on her own?

She clasped her arms around her knees and sat, thinking. Mr. Fluffypants stretched out across the bottom of the bed, his eyes closed, his paws kneading the air as he purred.

It'd been a couple of hours since she'd left Wyatt on the deck. She'd come to her room because there was nowhere else to go. She'd thought about calling Lily but didn't. Instead, she'd fallen asleep.

Now her belly growled, and she knew she was going to have to go out there. Dammit, why couldn't they have gone to Daddy's house? She'd never have to see Wyatt then. She could call the chef and get whatever she wanted. She could hole up with satellite television, Netflix, and gourmet food.

Instead, she was in close quarters with a seriously sexy and infuriating bodyguard. She couldn't avoid him all night. Especially if she wanted to eat.

It was still light out, but the sun had moved behind a mountain and the shadows were growing long. Paige climbed from the bed and Fluffy jumped down, running to the door.

"You little shit," she said. "You started the whole thing, you know."

He meowed and scratched at the door, oblivious. She opened it for him and then went into the bathroom to fix her hair and wipe the mascara from underneath her eyes before she followed the scent of food to the kitchen.

Wyatt looked up from where he was standing behind the counter, chopping a tomato. "Hey."

"Hey." Her heart throbbed at the sight of him. Why?

"Dinner is almost ready. If you're hungry."

"I am. What are we having? Or do I need to fix my own?" She wanted to bite her tongue after saying that last part. Why antagonize him?

"No, I got it. But you can carry this salad outside," he said, tossing the tomato into a bowl and holding it out.

Paige went over and took it from him. Their fingers brushed and her belly flipped. "Fluffypants is out and about," she said. "You might want to keep your bedroom door closed."

"Way ahead of you," he replied. He jerked his chin toward the closed doors to the deck. "Figured we'd eat outside. The view is too pretty to waste."

Paige carried the salad outside, making sure to shut the door behind her so Fluffy couldn't get out. The table was set with a cloth and silverware, though the plates were paper. There were also paper bowls—for the salad, she presumed. There was a wineglass for her and a bottle of water for him. A bottle of ranch salad dressing sat in the middle of the table.

Her heart swelled ridiculously, though it meant nothing. So he'd made a salad and dragged a bottle of ranch dressing loaded with preservatives from the pantry. It wasn't meant to be sweet. Wasn't meant as an apology. It was food.

He came outside behind her, carrying a pizza on a round stone. He set it in the middle of the table, and Paige felt a little bubble of happiness welling inside.

"It's just frozen pizza and bagged salad with a few extra veggies tossed in. If you don't like it, you can find something else."

Paige held up her hand in the universal stop gesture. "Don't ruin the moment, okay? You fixed dinner. Thank you."

He took a seat and she followed suit. "Yeah, well, it's from a box. Just thought you should know."

"That's not what I was talking about."

He reached for a slice of pizza and dragged it to her plate before getting his own. She dished out salad for them both and squeezed ranch onto hers. Then she mixed it up and took a bite.

It wasn't the best salad she'd ever had, but it didn't matter. The view more than made up for it. The light was golden, and the river was a dark ribbon slicing through the landscape instead of the sparkling one it had been earlier today.

Wyatt was watching her when she pulled her gaze back from the valley. She found herself panicking that maybe she'd gotten dressing all over her face or something.

"Nothing's wrong," he said, accurately reading her expression. "Just wondering if you were going to spit it out."

"I'm not *that* much of a snob."

"No, I guess not."

"You can't judge a book by its cover, Wyatt. I'm sure Mary Beth's told you that more than once."

"She has." He took a bite of the pizza and chewed.

Paige sighed. Was eating dinner worth this hassle? She could take it to her room and eat alone. Maybe it was better that way. She clearly annoyed him for some reason.

She started to push her chair back, but he reached out and covered her hand. The heat of him sizzled into her, making her nerves pop like jumping beans.

"Don't go." He blew out a breath. "I'm bad at this, Paige. Bad at being social, bad at knowing what to say, bad at holding in all the anger I'm carrying around. It's not your fault, and I know it. I don't mean to take it out on you."

She sank back into the chair and searched his gaze. He was so handsome that he made her tummy flip, and so serious her heart squeezed. What was going on in that brain of his?

"Okay."

"Eat. Please."

She took another bite of pizza. No, it wasn't artisan pizza fired in a wood oven, but it wasn't bad. The crust tasted like garlic. It was actually quite delicious.

"I'm sorry Mr. Fluffypants pooped on your bed. I don't know what got into him. And you're right that I shouldn't have told you to buy another comforter. He's my cat and my responsibility. I do clean his box at home. I scoop it every day, and I didn't today so he might have been protesting that rather than you. Your room is closer to the laundry room."

"I appreciate that."

"Did the, uh, stain come out?"

"It did."

"Do you need help making the bed?"

"I might."

She sighed. "Do you really want to have dinner with me or would you prefer to be alone? Because you don't have to entertain me, really. I can manage on my own."

"I'm not trying to entertain you. I'm trying to say I'm sorry for being an asshole earlier. I was pissed about the cat, but I crossed a line when I made it personal."

"Thank you."

"You're welcome."

They ate in silence for a few minutes as the shadows lengthened. She began to notice the forest sounds. Birds, crickets, frogs—and other things she probably couldn't identify. The air was cooler too.

"How's the pizza?" he asked.

She looked down at her empty plate and laughed. "Gone."

"You ate three pieces. I guess you didn't do that just to make me feel good for cooking dinner."

"No, guess not."

"There's ice cream."

"Really?"

"Yeah. You want some?"

"Maybe in a little bit. I think I'm too full." She hesitated. "I'm sorry about your friend, Wyatt."

He stiffened, his nostrils flaring. And then he relaxed, as if he'd given in to something. "Thanks."

She toyed with her wineglass. "If you want to talk—"

"I don't," he growled.

"Okay."

He swore as he raked a hand through his hair. "You know what? What the hell. Maybe it's time."

She held out a hand. "You don't have to. Don't do it unless you really want to."

He lifted an eyebrow. "Either you want to hear it or you don't."

"I do. But I don't want you to feel as if you have to tell me anything."

"This gonna end up on television?"

"What? No, of course not!"

He kicked his legs out as he leaned back against the seat. "I grew up in Eagle's Ridge, like I told you. Made the best friends a guy could ever have when we all got stuck in detention together in high school. Ryder, Adam, Zane, Noah, Jack, and Ford. All of us joined the military. Different branches, though Noah is a SEAL as well. Different team, however. We all left for different reasons. I love Eagle's Ridge, but I'm not as tied to it as Ryder or Adam and Zane. The others don't seem to be either. They're all out of the service or getting out, but only Noah is planning to come back. Ford and Jack live elsewhere."

He picked up his water and took a drink. She sipped at her wine, nervous about what he would say and also wanting to hear it.

"I should be telling them these things, and yet I'm contemplating telling you."

"I'm a stranger. Maybe it's easier."

"Maybe." He leaned forward, head turned and eyes on the scenery. "These guys are my best friends, the friends of my heart. But a guy makes friends with his teammates, and there was a dude I went through SEAL training with—"

He was silent for a long moment. Then he rocked back and held up two hands. "You know what, I don't want to do this."

"Then don't. You don't owe me an explanation."

He stood and went to the railing, his back to her. She sipped her wine.

"We were on the same team," he said after several

silent minutes. "We were on a recon mission, searching for a terrorist stronghold in the Hindu Kush—that's the high Afghan desert—when we were attacked. A sniper's bullet took out my friend. Danny was his name. He was standing beside me and then he wasn't. He had a wife and child—and I couldn't save him. It was too late."

Her throat was tight. "I'm sorry, Wyatt."

"It should have been me. If it had been me, Lisa and Emma would still have Danny."

"But Mary Beth wouldn't have you. Your friends wouldn't have you." *And neither would I.*

Paige swallowed. What the heck? She didn't have him now—didn't know him, not really—and didn't want him.

Well, okay, maybe she wanted him. In the most carnal sense of the word.

But that was different.

He didn't move for a long time. And then he nodded. Barely perceptible.

"Yeah. There's that."

She didn't know what to say. Didn't know the right words. But she knew what was in her heart.

"Did you know there would be a sniper that day?"

"No."

"Then you couldn't have stopped it, could you? What happened, happened."

He turned to her. His eyes raked over her. She thought she might have said something wrong. But then he put a hand over his eyes and shook his head before dropping it again.

"I've told myself the same thing a million times. But I still wonder if I could have changed it."

Instinct drove her to her feet. She crossed the distance between them and grasped his face in her hands. His eyes burned hot. Twin coals flaring brighter the longer she held him.

"If you could have changed it, you would have. But Mary Beth would be devastated. Your friends would be devastated. And I—" She choked. "Well, I would be in a shitload of trouble, because who would protect me from King?"

He reached up and laid his palm over her hand. His other hand went to her cheek, caressed it with infinite tenderness.

"I won't fail you, Paige. I won't let King near you."

"I know that."

He drew in a breath. His eyes burned bright. His hands tightened on her.

"I'm tempted to kiss you again, princess. But it's not a good idea because I don't know if I can stop this time."

"What if I don't want you to stop?"

The heat in his gaze flared and then banked. "Not a good idea to tempt me. Your safety is my priority. Getting involved could compromise my ability to protect you."

"Bullshit."

He stared at her for a long moment and then laughed. "Bullshit? Really? I thought you were more proper than that."

Paige cocked her head. "You've never seen *American Princess*, have you?"

"No. Why?"

"Because if you had, you'd know I'm not proper at all."

━━━

WYATT COULDN'T BELIEVE he'd told her as much as he had. But she was staring up at him with her fierce gaze, the gaze that said she believed in him, and he knew why he'd done it.

If he could tell someone who had no connection to him, no reason to be anything other than truthful with him, then maybe he could eventually tell his friends. He didn't feel any less guilty, not really, but somehow he felt a little better. He'd said the words to someone, and he hadn't fallen apart while doing it.

Maybe he could do it again. Maybe, if he said it enough, he'd start to believe there was nothing he could have done differently.

Her lips parted, her lashes dropped as she focused on his mouth, and his groin began to ache with need. He wanted to lose himself in her. But he couldn't.

"Paige."

"Wyatt."

She was cute as she gazed up at him expectantly.

"I want you. I really do. But we can't. Maybe when this is all over…"

But he knew it wouldn't happen then. She'd go back to Seattle, and he was staying right here in Eagle's Ridge. Going back to doing odd jobs and trying to find his footing again.

She sighed and he dropped his hands, taking a step backward. She crossed her arms over her chest and turned to the view. Her profile was lovely and sad.

"You're right. We hardly know one another, and these circumstances are far from normal. I'm sorry for putting you in a position you aren't comfortable with. And just so you know, I have *never*, not once, had an inappropriate relationship with a bodyguard. It's just…" She shook her head as if clearing it. "This doesn't seem like the usual bodyguard relationship to me. You don't act like a bodyguard."

"How do you mean?"

"You aren't distant and stuffy, you don't wear a black suit and carry a firearm in a shoulder holster beneath your jacket. You don't act like a typical tough guy. I think maybe you don't have to act like one—it's clear from your stance that you're somebody no one wants to mess with."

"You decided that in the past twenty-four hours?"

"I decided it in the first few seconds. It was the way you stood in my path at the airport, the way Bruce looked at you. You just seem so much more competent and, well, badass than any bodyguard I've ever had before." She waved a hand at him. "I can't tell where you'd put a firearm, and yet I'm sure you have one—"

"More than one. And a K-bar too."

"A K-bar?"

"A knife."

She smiled softly. "See? That's what I mean. You don't look armed and dangerous, but you are. That makes you kinda scary. It also makes me glad you're on my side. Maybe you should consider being a bodyguard full time. I'd hire you."

He shook his head. "I can't leave Gran again. I came home for her, so no. But thanks for the offer."

"I know Eagle's Ridge isn't huge, but there are tourists. My dad has property here. He can't be the only rich person who does. Maybe you could open a security firm of your own right here in town. Then you wouldn't have to leave at all."

He'd never thought of that before. But he also didn't think it would work. There couldn't be that big of a demand for personal security in Eagle's Ridge.

But there could be a demand for security in general.

Personal security, business security, event security. Yeah, there could be a demand. And he knew people. Friends who'd left the military. Not his best buddies who all had work of their own, but other former military Special Forces guys.

"Nah, I don't think there'd be enough work," he said even while his brain turned the idea over.

"You might be right." She gave him a bright smile. Maybe too bright. "Well, I suppose I should get online and tend my social media. I still have a brand to build, and a business deal to angle for. Thanks for dinner, Wyatt. It was lovely."

"You're welcome."

"If you need help making the bed, let me know."

"I will. Thanks."

"Yes, well, okay."

She stacked the plates and bowls they'd used, grabbed the silverware, and headed inside. He watched her go, hands stuffed in his jeans pockets, not moving as the sky darkened and the stars started to wink into existence.

Something had changed between them tonight. But whether it was good or bad, he couldn't say.

Chapter 15

"When are you coming back to the city, Paige?" Lily asked. "I miss you."

Paige frowned. It was raining hard and she'd been stuck indoors all day. Wyatt had his head buried in his computer and only grunted when she asked him questions. They hadn't been into town in two days now.

Dinner on the deck had been five nights ago. It was the last time she'd felt truly at ease with him. Since then, he'd treated her with a distant formality that had been infuriating until she got accustomed to it.

Hell, maybe she was still infuriated, but she was so busy trying to make a deal with different clothing manufacturers, from a distance, that she'd put it into the back of her mind.

"I don't know," Paige said in reply. "There's still no word on King."

"If you ask me, it's just a stunt. Maybe the studio did it for publicity. Do you think they could have done that?"

"I don't think so," Paige replied. "The police are involved, and whoever did it would end up in a lot of trouble, don't you think? Making false threats, wasting police time, et cetera."

Lily sighed. "I guess you're right."

Paige loved the girl who'd been her best friend since they were little and their dads were starting out together. Lily was sweet, but the elevator didn't always go to the top floor.

"Do you miss the show?" Paige asked. Because she wasn't the only one affected by the hiatus. There were five of them, but Paige only cared about her and Lily. None of them needed the money, but several of them wanted the fame.

"Not really," Lily replied. "I hate all the fighting. You know that."

"I know. So you'd be happy if it didn't come back?"

Lily sighed. "It wouldn't upset me, but I would be unhappy for you. I know you want it very badly."

Paige was torn. Yes, she wanted the show back. She wanted to be a household name because that would get her what she ultimately wanted. But she knew how much shy Lily hated the spotlight. Lily had only agreed to be on the show because Paige had talked her into it.

More like begged, truth be told. The producers had wanted five women, not four, and they wanted Lily and Paige as a package deal since their fathers famously worked together. Since Lily's father had bought an equal interest in SpenTech a few years ago, when Paige's dad was rumored to be nearing bankruptcy, there'd been tension at the company. Because of that, the producers had expected more drama between the women.

The only drama that had ever been between them, however, was the manufactured drama the producers forced on them. After each taping, they were back to being best friends. Whatever messes their fathers had made, it didn't affect them.

"It's not the show I want," Paige said truthfully. "It's the influence."

"You should ask your dad for the money, Paige. He'd give it to you."

He wouldn't, but she wasn't going to argue with Lily. Lily's dad would give her anything she wanted, and no strings attached either. But not Paige's dad.

"It's not the same, Lil. I have to do this myself. My dad is self-made. I want to be self-made." Even if she knew she had advantages simply by being a Spencer.

But so far, those advantages hadn't translated into any deals.

"We need to go to Paris," Lily said. "I need a new handbag, and I want to see the new collections. I don't want what everyone else has."

There was a time when Paige would have jumped on that idea, but something about the whole notion of flying to Paris to pick out an expensive handbag—and probably a whole new wardrobe too—seemed wrong. She stared at the rain coming down, the lushness of the green mountains cloaked in gray, and felt strangely disconnected from her life in Seattle.

She'd gone to watch Mary Beth ride the last time they'd gone to town. Wyatt had stood there completely stony-faced while his grandmother tacked up her admittedly giant horse. She'd used a mounting block to get on the beast.

And then, amazingly enough, Zeus tucked his head and did absolutely everything she asked of him without much of a complaint. Paige had thought, watching Mary Beth from the sidelines, that you'd never know she was seventy-eight. Or that she was battling diabetes. She wasn't a large woman, but she had built up a bit of weight around the middle, and that made for insulin-resistance. Riding was one of the ways she was trying to combat it.

It had been peaceful being around horses again. The smells, the snorts, the grace and beauty of the animals. Paige'd had a strong desire to find the nearest tack store and buy a pair of jodhpurs and boots so she could ride too.

"We'll go soon, I promise," Paige said. Because once she got back to her life, she'd settle right in again. All these feelings of discontent would disappear. Eagle's Ridge would fade from memory, and so would Wyatt. She felt a twinge of sadness at that thought, but she tamped it down firmly.

She didn't even like it here, not really. She tolerated it. She adapted to her surroundings. She wouldn't miss a thing about it when she left.

Outside, the rain fell steadily. A deer emerged from the woods farther down the slope and ambled across the open ground. A baby followed, its white spots so cute as it frolicked after its mother.

A week ago, she'd never even seen a deer in person. Now she'd seen so many she'd lost track. And each time one strolled across the grass, her heart leaped with happiness at the sight.

Didn't mean she wasn't going to be happy to get home again, up high in her penthouse apartment overlooking the Sound. There was no wildlife there, no random deer sightings. But there *was* food delivery, gourmet restaurants, the best coffee in the world, and more entertainment than any one person could consume.

Seattle was heaven. She couldn't wait to get back to it.

"I can't wait," Lily said. "Let's go now. You can bring your bodyguard. What's the difference if you're in Paris or wherever they've stashed you? It's still a long way from Seattle."

"I can't right now." Because Wyatt wasn't going to Paris. Even if she successfully managed to talk everyone involved in her case into letting her go overseas, it would be with a different bodyguard. Something about that idea opened up a pit in her belly.

"For all I know, you're in Paris now," Lily said. "Why won't you tell me where you are? I could visit."

"I'm not in Paris, honey. I haven't even left the state, okay? But I can't leave here right now."

She hadn't told Lily about Wyatt. She'd meant to, but something always held her back. Like talking about him was wrong. Which was silly. Talking about a man she was attracted to wasn't a crime, especially when there was nothing going on between them.

But still she didn't say anything. Her phone began to buzz with another call. She glanced at it. She didn't recognize the number, but she'd been taking so many calls from various potential business partners lately that it didn't matter. Besides, she wanted to put an end to this conversation before it got any more uncomfortable.

"I have to go, Lily. I have an important call coming in. I'll talk to you soon, okay? Hugs and kisses!" She flashed over to the other call. "This is Paige."

"Hello, my queen. Where have you been hiding?"

———

PAIGE'S VOICE lifted the hairs on the back of Wyatt's neck. She'd been in her room all morning, on the phone, but this time she was shouting. He got to his feet and strode toward her door, alarm coursing through him. Not enough to burst in on her, but enough to see what the hell was happening.

Probably just a bad meeting, but he had to check.

"Paige," he shouted as he rapped on the door. "Open up."

A moment later the door flew open and she stood there in yoga pants and a sweatshirt. Her hair was in a ponytail —and her face was as white as a sheet.

He didn't even hesitate. He gathered her against him. She didn't stiffen or pull away. She wrapped her arms around him and melted against his body.

"What's wrong, baby?"

She trembled from head to toe and his alarm grew. He pushed her back gently. Wide hazel eyes shimmering with tears gazed up at him.

"He called me, Wyatt. He has my number."

Ice washed over him. "King called you?"

"Yes."

Fury rolled like a wave of fire over his body. "I need your phone."

"It's on the bed."

He set her gently away and went over to collect her phone. He brought up the last call. If the man was smart, the number was a burner. But not everyone was smart.

"What did he say?"

She pushed a lock of hair that had fallen from her ponytail away from her face. "He said I couldn't hide from him forever. That he'd find me. That we're destined to be together."

Rage rolled through him. Wyatt took Paige's hand, and she followed him into the living room where he collected his phone from the table. He dialed Hawk.

"Yeah, man?"

"Paige got a call on her cell. I have a number for you."
He rattled it off when Hawk gave him the go ahead.

"I'll get a trace on it. What did he say to her?"

"The usual crazy bullshit assholes like this say. They're destined to be together and he'll find her."

"I'll let you know what we get on this number as soon as I have something."

"Thanks."

He ended the call and set the phone down. Then he gathered Paige in his arms again. He'd spent the last few days purposely not touching her. Not letting himself give in to the urge to talk to her more than was necessary. He'd been cool and distant, but now that he'd held her again it was impossible to let her go.

So he let himself do it. For now.

She wrapped her arms around him and held on tight. They didn't speak at first.

"You okay?" he asked her.

She nodded.

"Did he say anything else?"

"Not really. Nothing that stands out. I started yelling at him. And then I hung up when you knocked on the door."

"He's never called you before, right?"

"No."

"He got your number from somewhere. From some*one*. This is somebody who knows you, Paige. Or knows someone in your circle."

"I meet a lot of people. I don't give many my number. But—God, I've been talking to so many people lately, so many executives at different companies, that I thought it was one of them returning my call. How am I supposed to try to run a business if I can't even answer my own damned phone?"

Her fingers curled into his shirt. She was warm and

fragile in his arms. He wanted to slay dragons for her. But first he needed to find the dragon.

"I think it's time I watched your show," he said.

She pushed back to look up at him. "I wish you wouldn't."

He cocked an eyebrow. "Why not?"

"Because I'm a total bitch on the show. I'm outrageous and, well, not the real me. It's mostly scripted, no matter that it's a reality show."

"Still, I need to see the dynamics. And you need to tell me about the people who work on the show behind the scenes."

She sighed. "Surely they've been checked. The police have a list of everyone who works there, from the production assistants to the security guards. There are a lot of people, Wyatt."

He pushed her hair off her face, let himself enjoy skimming his fingers over her smooth skin.

"Between the photo at your apartment building and today's call on your personal number, I'm more convinced than ever it's someone in your circles. If this guy was a random crank, it would have never escalated beyond the letters sent to the studio. But he's not random. He knows you."

She shivered in his arms. He should let her go, but he didn't want to.

"Okay, yes, you have to be right. But I still don't know who it could be."

"Then pull up Netflix and let's have an *American Princess* marathon."

She looked uncertain. "Watching the series won't show you the people behind the scenes."

"It won't. But it may spark questions I haven't thought of yet."

"I still wish you wouldn't."

He put a finger under her chin, tipped it up until he could gaze into her eyes. She didn't flinch from the look he gave her. "What are you afraid of, Paige? That I won't like you?"

"Pretty much."

"I don't think that's possible," he said, his gaze dropping to her mouth. A mouth he wanted to do things to.

His groin started to throb, and he jerked his attention back to her pretty eyes. She was watching him with an invitation in her gaze. He very much wanted to accept it. But he set her away from him instead.

"I already like you far too much."

Chapter 16

Paige wanted to squirm. It was uncomfortable watching herself be a bitch. She'd never had trouble with the episodes in the past—had studied them relentlessly—but now they made her uneasy.

Probably because the man sitting nearby didn't say much. He'd slouched in his seat, drink near his hand, elbow on the arm of the sofa and his fingers near his mouth as he studied the screen.

After every episode, he'd queue up the next one. There were ten of them, forty minutes without commercials. Almost seven hours of privileged women prancing across the screen and getting into catfights over the most inane thing, or acting stupid because the viewers liked to think they were better than the people on-screen in some way. There were lunches, dinners, shopping trips where they spent ridiculous amounts of money.

There was also dating. Paige had only gone on one date so far. That was the one with Donnie Warren. There hadn't been any real sparks, but they'd pretended for the cameras. Wyatt hadn't gotten to that episode yet.

Paige was the one the others loved to hate. She refused to play stupid over anything, and they despised her for it. Except for Lily, who only pretended to be upset with her. The other princesses had meetings behind her back, complained about her, made plans to cut her from their lives. Servants strolled in and out of the frame, and that was when Wyatt seemed to pay even more attention.

"Who's that guy?" he'd ask.

"Oh, that's John. He's an actor," she'd say. Or some variation on that sentence each and every time. Sometimes the servants were real. The waiters and waitresses in restaurants were often real, though not always.

"So he's not been on the show again?" Wyatt would ask from time to time.

"No. He was there for that episode. Haven't seen him again."

After five episodes, Paige couldn't take it another moment. As Wyatt let the next episode start to load, she got to her feet.

"Can we take a break? Please?"

He looked up at her with serious eyes. "I need to see these, Paige."

"You don't have to see every single episode back to back. Let's take a break. Please, I'm begging you."

He finally nodded and pressed the Stop button. "Okay."

She paced away from him, toward the kitchen, her stomach burning with shame and anger.

"What's wrong, Paige?"

When she whirled around, Wyatt was there, looking concerned.

Her feelings bubbled over like a pot of water left too long. She flung her arms wide. "I'm just sick of watching, okay? I thought—I thought I was getting somewhere in my career with the show. I had all those meetings with people —and not one of them took a chance on me. I watched every episode when it aired, and I never saw the patronizing expressions those men and women had before. Why didn't I know they weren't taking me seriously? Why didn't I see they were making fun of me?"

"I don't think they were making fun of you, Paige. I think they were listening to you but having a hard time reconciling the brain inside the pretty head."

He held up a hand when she started to protest.

"I'm not saying it's fair or right. I'm not saying I agree. I'm saying they judged you based on the cover. They never opened the book. That's their fault, not yours."

She put her forehead in her hand and shook her head. "I thought being over the top and outrageous would get me what I wanted. I thought the more attention I garnered, the more fans I'd gain. And then at least one of these manufacturers would see that and want to take a chance on my clothing line. But every one of them looked at me like I was wasting their time."

"So you'll prove to them you weren't."

Her lip trembled and she bit it. Dammit, it wasn't like her to cry. She was stronger than this. "How?"

His mouth flattened as he considered it. He didn't know either, and that just made her feel even more despair than she already did.

And yet she needed to suck it up, didn't she? She still had more money and privilege than most. She could find a way to do this.

"Put on your shoes, Paige."

"Why?"

"Because you need to get out for a while. I'm taking you to town."

EAGLE'S RIDGE bustled with activity. It wasn't raining in town anymore, though it had still been raining on the mountain when they'd come down. It was humid in the valley, and Paige was glad she'd opted for a sundress and sandals. She had a small sweater balled up in her purse in case she got cool, but it didn't look very likely just yet.

Wyatt took her to the town square. There was a big park not too far distant, and all the buildings facing the square were from the 1950s and 60s. There were cute little shops in some of them—an art gallery and an antique store as well as a hair salon and photography studio. There was also a coffee shop, a wine store, and a pizza joint. Hildie's House was on the other side, in a quaint cottage with a front porch that ran the width of the house.

In the park, people were busy putting up bunting and a crew hung American flags from all the lampposts. There was a gathering of carnival trucks with rides in a nearby parking lot.

"They're getting ready for the July Fourth celebration. The carnival will set up tomorrow and run all weekend. The event culminates with a big fireworks display on the evening of the Fourth. There'll be a parade through downtown, and booths on display around the square with local crafts and food."

"Sounds like fun."

"If you're still here, we can stop by. Probably safer to watch the fireworks from the mountain though."

If she was still here? The celebration was still a few days away, so it was possible the police would catch the guy harassing her and she'd be free to leave. A twinge of sadness hit her at the thought.

What if she wasn't ready to go?

Wasn't ready to go? Of course she was! She had a life to live in Seattle, a company to get off the ground—she couldn't do those things from this tiny little place, no matter how pretty.

Wyatt caught her hand as they walked. "Hildie's around somewhere," he said. "I can feel her eyes on us."

Paige would have laughed except she kind of liked that he'd grabbed her hand. She wished it was because he wanted to, not because of the town gossip and the idea she was supposed to be his visiting girlfriend rather than a client.

He led them toward the Snake River where it cut the town in two. The path was pretty even though it was wet, and the sound of the river roiling against the banks was more peaceful than she'd have thought it could be.

The other side of the river was where Mary Beth lived. Paige almost suggested visiting Wyatt's grandmother but thought maybe that was pushing it a little far. She liked Mary Beth, but she didn't want to spend more time with her as if they were going to remain a part of each other's lives. She suspected that Mary Beth wouldn't mind, but the thing was that Paige would. Mary Beth was motherly in a way that Paige had never had. It made her want to cling, and that wasn't a good thing.

"Feeling any better?" Wyatt asked after they'd been walking along the river path for a while.

"Better, yes. But I still don't have a solution."

He stopped and pulled her over to the railing where they could gaze down at the river.

"Maybe you're looking at it wrong. Maybe you need to consider some different angles. You wanted to find a manufacturer to partner with you, correct?"

"Yes. I've had some test clothing made, but I need someone who is good at distribution and economies of scale. I could get everything made in China, but I don't want to do that. It's not the same quality, for one thing. I need a partner with the warehouses and the distribution connections. I need to know the timelines on production."

"Why don't you partner with a retailer? The Pioneer Woman sells cookware in Walmart. Which do you think came first? She found the pots and pans, or she partnered with the retailer who could source that for her?"

Paige frowned. It wasn't that she hadn't thought of the retailer option, but she felt like having the production in place would make it an easier sell. She wasn't the Pioneer Woman. That was what a hit show and a huge audience could do for you.

"I don't think it matters. She had the audience to justify it—and Walmart came to her, I'd bet. She didn't go to them."

"So how do you make them come to you?"

"I was trying to do that with the show."

"Think about it for a second. The Pioneer Woman cooks. Walmart sells pots and pans. You want to sell clothing—but you were on a reality show about spoiled heiresses. Why would anyone want to buy clothes from you?"

She frowned. "Because I wore really cute clothes on the show! And I styled some of the girls too. Everyone loved my outfits."

"You need *Project Runway*, not *American Princess*. Or you need to adjust your expectations. When we planned a mission in the SEALs, it sometimes took months. We'd go over every aspect of the intelligence, formulate a hundred ways it could work, test fire a metric ton of bullets, do live fire drills, and we'd run test scenarios again and again. We'd analyze the data, formulate a plan—with backup plans—and then we'd go. And honey, that's even when we didn't know we had a mission coming."

"How do you practice a mission when you don't know it's coming?"

He grinned. "Exactly. But you do, because you have to be ready. It's more about the techniques. You have to know how to behave in every possible situation. So you game it. Over and over and over. Until you can do it in your sleep. That's what you have to do. Keep gaming it, keep working on it. Explore scenarios and test them all. One of them will work. You just don't know which one yet."

She could only stare at him. Then she laughed. "I feel like I just climbed a mountain to see a guru and he gave me the vaguest answer possible. A total nonanswer that fixes nothing. The answer is within," she intoned. "Look inside yourself for the truth."

He laughed. "Sorry. But I can't fix it for you. I said you needed a show focused on fashion rather than one focused on a lifestyle most women don't have access to. That's the best I can do."

The truth, when it hit her, was a hammer.

"Wait a minute. That's it. You're right." She couldn't believe she'd missed it before. "It's not *American Princess* at all. I need to show women how to make their lives better, not be so outrageous in mine that I hope it gets me fans so I can *then* show them how to make their lives better."

"So how do you do that?"

"Oh my God. I'm an idiot."

"Wow, never thought I'd hear you say that. Are you sure you're feeling okay?"

She swatted at him. He didn't duck and her hand felt like it hit iron. Okay, that was some arm he had there. As if she didn't know it. He'd held her close only a little while ago. She'd swooned in those arms. Enjoyed it too.

"I'm fine. But I can't believe I didn't think of this." Excitement bubbled in her veins. "I have the money to produce some pretty high quality video. Not a show, no way—but videos for YouTube? Yes, I can do that. I thought YouTube was too narrow for what I wanted. I thought the distribution that *American Princess* had would give me a bigger audience. And it *will*. But not the right audience, or not an audience tuning in for lifestyle tips. But if I make them myself—nice production values, quality tips —on my own channel, I can reach more women that way. Some will tune in because of the show. But if a video goes viral, it'll get more eyes on it. Eventually I'll hit the right audience."

Wyatt whistled. "Damn, girl. All that from a walk by the river. Maybe you need to get out of Seattle a bit more often."

She smiled. It felt like it would bust at the edges it was so wide. Relief coursed through her. Maybe she wouldn't succeed this way either, but maybe she would. Maybe she needed to stop being in such a hurry and concentrate on practicing scenarios.

Paige flung her arms around his neck. He caught her but didn't push her away.

"Thank you, Wyatt. You've made me see what I was doing wrong. I think I have a way forward now."

His arms tightened around her. "I like it when you smile," he said, and her heart did a somersault.

"You're just saying that so I won't give you that bad bodyguard review."

He chuckled. "Yeah, I'm so worried about my reviews."

Standing in his arms was intoxicating. She should probably pull away, but she didn't want to. "Do you think you might kiss me again? Just to celebrate, of course."

He tugged her closer, until she could feel the hard lines of his body pressing into hers.

"I think I shouldn't… but I think I'm gonna do it anyway."

Chapter 17

The second their lips touched, fireworks started zinging in his gut, his brain, his heart. And his groin. Most definitely in his groin.

It had been a long time since Wyatt had been this juiced over a woman. Since he'd wanted to strip her naked and spend time exploring all the curves and valleys of her body.

There was just something about Paige Spencer that got to him on a primal level. It was screwed up, no doubt about it, because they were from such different lives that even if he wanted to date her, he never could.

But as their mouths melded and her warm body stepped into his, as the space between them disappeared, everything that was wrong about the situation dropped away. All he cared about was getting more of this adrenaline rush.

He cupped her jaw in both hands, slanted his mouth over hers, and took everything she gave him. His dick was rock solid. His heart slammed against his ribs. Desire beat a drum inside his brain.

Take her, take her, take her.

He wanted to. But they were in Eagle's Ridge, in the middle of the park, and it wasn't possible. Which was good, really, because it meant he could regain his senses.

Paige's arms wrapped around his neck, her body arched into his, and she made little noises in her throat that drove him wild.

"Looks like it may work out this time," a voice said, and Wyatt groaned inwardly.

"Hello, Mrs. Fontana," he said as he set Paige away from him, arm wrapped loosely around her waist to steady her. And to keep her close enough to hide the massive hard-on she'd given him.

She blinked up at him—he could see the instant the fog cleared. She whipped around to stare at Hildie.

"Hi," Paige said.

Hildie Fontana stood there in one of her caftans, her long silver hair clipped back in a barrette, big paste jewels winking from her fingers, smiling like she'd just stumbled onto a secret cache of weapons.

Or maybe that was him who smiled big when stumbling on weapons caches.

Dammit, think.

"We were just enjoying the cool evening," he said.

Hildie's eyebrows did that dance thing they did. "I can see that, yes. So how about coming over to the shop sometime to see the estate jewelry, hmm? You could find something for your lovely Nicole. To commemorate this time in your relationship."

"Yes, I'll do that. We'll do that."

"When are you going back to Virginia, Nicole?"

"Oh, uh, after the holiday."

Hildie clapped her hands like a child who'd just been

given a treat. "Wonderful! You're going to love our celebration, dear. So much patriotism and fun. I promise you've never experienced its like anywhere else."

Wyatt didn't bother to tell Hildie that he'd spent at least two Fourths in Washington DC, celebrating on the National Mall with the fireworks exploding around the Washington Monument. He was pretty sure that one was a bit grander than Eagle's Ridge.

But they still put on a hell of a show for a small town.

"I can't wait."

"Well," Hildie said. "I have to get moving. The dogs are waiting to go out." She pointed at Wyatt. "You bring this lovely girl to the shop before she goes home."

"I will. Thank you."

Hildie bustled off and Wyatt shook his head. "Well, damn. Wonder what the rumor will be now."

Paige laughed. "It can't get any worse, can it? According to your grandmother, she was going to have us expecting by the end of the first day she met me. Did she? Do you know?"

Wyatt frowned. "I don't know. I don't *want* to know. It was bad enough to think she'd have us engaged."

It was Paige's turn to frown. "Oh, come on, really? Worried I'm going to cramp your style, stud?"

He caught her hand and dragged her into him. Maybe he shouldn't do it, but she made his heart feel lighter than it had in a long time.

"Forget Hildie and her meddling. Think about how happy you were just a few moments ago. You found a new way to solve your problem."

She smiled up at him. "I did. But I have another problem I'm not sure how to solve."

"What's that?"

"You, Wyatt. It's not fair for you to kiss me and leave me in this state."

"What state?" He knew what state. He was in it too.

"Flustered. Hot. Unsatisfied."

He sighed. "I told you why we can't do anything about it."

"Bull. I don't believe for two seconds that your ability to protect me will be compromised. You haven't stopped thinking about my safety. You *won't* stop thinking about it. It's ingrained in you, Wyatt. You're a SEAL."

He gazed down at her, his desire warring with his brain. His head told him not to do this. Not to get involved with her, no matter how lovely she was or how much he wanted her. His dick said do it. Because she was right, he wasn't going to fail to put her safety first.

He'd failed to save Danny, but he and Danny were equals on the field of battle. He hadn't been protecting Danny the way he was protecting Paige. He wouldn't stop doing his job if they were intimate.

"Still not sure it's a good idea," he told her. "I need my head clear, not tangled up with thoughts about how to get you naked."

Her smile heated his blood by several degrees.

"I can tell you how, Wyatt. Just ask me. That's all you need to do."

***

BY THE TIME they got back up the mountain, he was all in. There was something exciting about Paige. She made him feel things he hadn't felt in a long time. That had to be worth something, right?

But he wasn't going to forget what his primary responsibility was. When they reached the house, it was after dark. He checked the perimeter on his phone before turning off the truck. It hadn't been breached, but he wasn't finished with securing the premises.

"Wait here," he told her, drawing his weapon and clearing the house. The only thing waiting inside was Mr. Fluffypants, looking indignant and maybe hungry. "I get her first," he said to the cat. "You get her when I'm done. Understand?"

Mr. Fluffypants meowed, but Wyatt wasn't certain if it was agreement or protest. He strode back outside and went over to open Paige's door. She turned toward him, that little sundress slipping up her legs, and he stopped her with two hands on her knees.

Then he ran his palms up her bare thighs, enjoying the smoothness of her skin. The heat. He wanted to slip a thumb beneath her panties and feel her slick flesh. But he didn't. There was plenty of time for that.

She gazed at him with heavy-lidded eyes. When she bit her lower lip, he nearly groaned. Instead, he tugged her toward him. Her legs opened. He slid her against him until her silky panties were flush with his jeans-clad groin.

They stared at each other for a long moment. And then he speared a hand into her hair, cupping the back of her head, bringing her mouth to his.

She melted. Her arms went around his neck, her back arched, her crotch fitting tightly to his. He could feel her heat against him, and he knew he wanted to be buried inside her.

The kiss was scorching, but he hadn't expected anything less. Tongues tangled, breaths mingled, bodies strained toward each other.

Wyatt picked her up, and she wrapped her legs around

his waist as he gripped her bottom and kicked the truck door closed. He carried her to the house, bumped the door open with a foot, and walked inside without breaking the kiss.

But he had to break it to lock the door and set the alarm with his phone. Paige took that opportunity to feather kisses over his jaw and neck. When he had everything locked down tight, he turned his attention back to her.

She was a grenade to the brain, her body a lethal weapon she'd lobbed into his space. He wanted nothing more than to watch her detonate. He couldn't refuse her, even though a corner of his mind told him he should.

He wasn't going to, however. He was aroused. She was the only woman to arouse him in months, and he wasn't taking that lightly. Maybe Paige was the way back. The return to the land of the living.

He set her on the floor and reached for the hem of her dress. But then he stopped and frowned down at her.

Her pretty hazel eyes were glazed. They cleared quickly though.

"What?"

"Just wondering if this is what you really want."

"Sex? With you?" She nodded. "Yes, it's exactly what I want."

His gut tightened and his heart soared at the same time. "Is this because you figured out the YouTube thing?" he teased.

"Of course. I always get hot and bothered over the mention of YouTube."

He wanted to laugh. "You're naughty, Paige."

"I know. Want to spank me?"

Holy shit, she made him hard. "I might," he growled. "But first I want to get you naked."

He lifted the hem of her sundress up her thighs, her waist, her breasts. She raised her arms and he dragged the dress up and off.

"Whoa," he said.

She wore a white bra and panties, and he'd never seen anything so pretty in his life. Her underwear was plain with a little bit of lace trim, but it was somehow sexier on her than any thong he'd ever seen.

"Your turn to remove something."

"Go ahead," he told her, holding his arms out. He thought she'd go for his shirt, but she unbuckled his belt instead. Then she dragged it free and dropped it. Her eyes were twin flames as she met his gaze. She flicked open the button on his fly, and his body responded.

A loud meow burst up from below. Paige squeaked and jumped at the same time. Then she glared down at the creature lurking at her feet.

"Fluffy! Not *now*," she said.

Wyatt couldn't help but laugh. He shouldn't laugh at a time like this, and yet he found himself amused anyway.

"Go ahead and feed him," he said. Because the damned cat wouldn't leave them alone if she didn't. He knew enough about the creature to realize that.

"I'm sorry."

He caught her wrist as she started to turn away. "I'm not." He reached around and unhooked her bra. She gasped, her eyes wide. He pulled it from her shoulders and tossed it onto the couch.

Her breasts were a wet dream come true. Firm, round, with upturned nipples he wanted to lick. Instinctively, she put her hands over them. He gently pulled them away.

"Feed the cat. I want to watch."

She arched an eyebrow. "Who's naughty now?"

"Me. Definitely me. I don't mind admitting it."

She turned on her heel and walked over to the kitchen where she proceeded to get a can of cat food and pop the top. She grabbed a spoon, grabbed the cat's bowl, and upended the can.

Her breasts jiggled the entire time, and Wyatt's body responded with an aching hardness that he wasn't sure would ever be satisfied.

The cat meowed and purred and twisted himself around Paige's legs. Lucky beast.

She glanced up at him and gave him a wicked grin. Then she dropped to her haunches and set the bowl on the floor. Fluffy dived in, all else forgotten. Paige straightened and washed her hands. Then she strolled toward him again.

Wyatt forgot to breathe for a moment. When she reached him, he cupped her breasts in both hands, feeling the smoothness of them. Paige bit her lip as he skated a thumb over each nipple.

"You like that," he said.

"Of course I do."

"I intend to do a lot more than touch them."

"Oh, I hope so." She sidled closer, her fingers finding his zipper. He ached to be free, and his breath shortened as he waited.

She hesitated, frowning.

"What?"

"Fluffy. If we don't close a door, he's going to be a colossal pain in the ass."

"Like he isn't already," Wyatt said.

But he didn't wait for a solution. Instead, he bent and caught her around the knees, lifting her into his arms. Then he carried her to the master, kicking the door closed behind him before setting her down again.

"Where were we?"

She laughed. And then she grabbed his zipper and began to ease it downward. "Here, I think."

Chapter 18

Paige's heart galloped like a racehorse as she tugged Wyatt's zipper down. She asked herself a million questions all at once. Things like: Am I ready for this? Is it really what I want? Am I crazy? What if this makes it awkward between us? What if I like him too much? What if he doesn't like me? What if it's only physical?

But then the zipper reached the bottom and his dick pressed against his underwear and all thoughts fled as she palmed him. He was hot and hard, and her insides melted.

She glanced up, met his eyes, and her lungs stopped working for a long moment.

"You're beautiful," he said.

"So are you."

His gaze dropped and her nipples tightened. "You have no idea the things I want to do to you."

"I'd like to find out."

One corner of his mouth lifted in a sexy grin. "Then today is your lucky day."

He caught her to him, fused his mouth to hers. She'd

wanted to be in control, wanted to slide his jeans off his hips and then reveal his body slowly.

But he was having none of it.

She should have known. He was a SEAL. A hardened military man accustomed to being in control. There was no way he was ceding that territory to her.

Paige sighed as she gave herself over to it. To him. He would take care of her. Cherish her, at least for this. He wasn't going to be rough or fast. Not this time.

She might like fast and rough with him sometime, but first they had to take it slow and get to know each other.

He lifted her like she weighed nothing and set her back on the bed. Then he came down on top of her, still fully dressed except for the vee in his jeans where she'd pushed them open.

She, on the other hand, only had on a pair of panties. It was sensual and exciting to lie beneath him with the roughness of his clothing on her naked skin. To feel like she was utterly at his mercy but also that she was safe and protected.

He kissed her until she was a puddle of happiness, and then he trailed kisses down her neck and chest until his mouth fastened on a nipple. She thought she would come unglued with a single tug on her sensitive flesh, but she miraculously didn't. He licked and sucked until she was a mass of nerves, until her fingers curled into his shoulders and her breath came in little pants.

When she thought she couldn't take the anticipation anymore, he moved over and did the same to her other nipple until she was ready to sob with need. Finally he continued the journey downward until he was running his tongue along the waistband of her panties.

"You want me to keep going?" he asked.

She couldn't breathe. "If you don't, I'll record your

negative review and distribute it to news outlets. I'll skip the website entirely. You'll never work again."

He snorted. "I'd love to challenge you on that one, but the truth is you won't have to." He hooked his thumbs into the waistband of her panties and dragged them down her hips and over her ankles before throwing them on the floor. "I have every intention of going here," he said, skimming his fingers over her heated flesh.

He teased her first, kissing and licking everywhere but the place she wanted him most. Finally, when she was wound tighter than a spring, he touched his tongue to her.

"Ohhhh," she groaned as sparks flared behind her eyelids.

Wyatt spread her with his thumbs as his tongue pressed against her clit. Paige squirmed as he circled and nibbled and sucked. She could feel the crisis building, but it wasn't happening.

It wasn't happening because Wyatt seemed to know it was coming and he did everything he could to prolong it.

"Please," she finally begged. "Please."

"You want to come?"

"Yes!"

He slipped a finger inside her. And then he performed a full frontal assault on her body with his tongue and teeth and fingers, strumming her into a quivering, aching mess.

Paige didn't slip over the edge. She hurtled over it, screaming the whole way down, gasping for air as her body imploded. She landed in a mass of nerves, her body still zinging, her limbs going limp with pleasure, her heart racing as if she'd run up the mountain.

She thought he would strip now, slide his way into her, pump them both to another pinnacle. He didn't. Instead, he began the slow buildup again, licking his way to her center, spreading her open with his thumbs, lightly touching her still-sensitive clit.

"No," she moaned. "I can't."

"I think you can."

He took his time, but he proved that she could. This time when it was finished, when her limbs refused to work and she lay against the pillows and thought about a nap, he stood and reached for his T-shirt hem with one hand, dragged it up and off until that magnificent chest was on display.

Paige perked up. She was still suffering the aftershocks of his sensual assault, thinking she couldn't possibly have another orgasm for hours, when the sight of his chest set off a new current of desire within.

When he shoved his jeans and underwear down his hips, her breath caught. His penis sprang free, hard and beautiful, and Paige thought she'd never wanted a man so much in her life. Especially since she was already perfectly satisfied.

But oh, he was lovely. She wanted to lick him. She sat up, reaching for him, but he backed just out of reach.

"Not this time. I want to be inside you."

He produced a condom from his wallet, and she thanked God for men who came prepared. Then he rolled it on and sank down on top of her again. He didn't let his body touch hers yet, however. He held himself up on those strong arms of his, hovering over her, and she shivered at the heat in those eyes.

She ran her hands over the muscles of his arms, over his pectorals, marveling at how gorgeous he was. How amazing his body. These muscles weren't carved in a gym, though he probably kept them honed in one.

No, these muscles had been carved during intense military training. She couldn't imagine everything he'd seen.

Her heart ached as she thought of what he'd told her earlier about his friend.

"Wyatt," she breathed, because her heart was full and she couldn't say anything else.

"I need you to know something, Paige. I need you to know that I haven't spent the past few months in Eagle's Ridge picking up women and screwing around. You're my first since I left the Navy. I'm not sure why that is, but it's the truth."

She threaded her fingers into his hair. "Thank you for telling me."

But part of her wished she didn't know, because it made this more special than it should be. For her, anyway. She didn't want to get attached to him, but she was. She already knew it.

He lowered himself slowly, by degrees, and then he took her mouth. She opened to him eagerly, her mouth and her body, lifting her hips and wrapping her legs around his thighs.

He pressed against her entrance, solid and large, and then he kept on pressing until he filled her. Until they were joined together in the most intimate way possible.

"You okay?" he asked.

"I will be." It was the truth. He was big and it had been a long time, but her body was quickly adjusting.

"You ready?"

"Yes."

He began to move, withdrawing slowly and then pushing back in. Sensation streaked through her at every movement of his body inside hers. She didn't remember sex being so thrilling, but with him it was. At a certain point, with anyone else, it had seemed like something you had to do in order to get the reward.

With Wyatt, sex *was* the reward. An orgasm was merely icing on the cake.

It didn't take long before he was moving hard and fast, hips rising and falling into her again and again. Paige couldn't stop the low moans coming from her throat as he slammed into her, drawing all the nerves in her body into that one tight point as the base of his cock rubbed against her clit over and over.

And then she exploded as she had before, but somehow it was more intense this time. Wyatt didn't stop stroking into her, didn't stop drawing every ounce of pleasure from her that he could get. When she was spent and trembling, he thrust one last time, groaning as he came deep inside her.

He propped himself on his elbows, his body still joined to hers, and kissed her leisurely. As if he had all the time in the world. Paige arched into him and gave him everything she had.

"That was amazing," he whispered against her lips. Then he levered up and went to the bathroom. She assumed he was taking care of the condom.

She stretched and yawned. The sheets felt so sensual against her skin. The covers were warm, her body sated. Her belly growled, but who needed food at a time like this?

There was a meow on the other side of the closed door and then a scratch on the wood. Paige sat up.

Wyatt strode from the bathroom, his naked body on display for her viewing pleasure. He was so at ease in his skin whereas she'd drawn the covers up to hide her breasts. She wasn't ashamed of her body, but she was shy now that they'd been intimate.

And she was confused, because what did it mean?

Does it need to mean anything?

No, it didn't. She wasn't typically a sex for sex's sake

kind of girl, but she often wished she was. Usually she needed to be in a relationship—so this was an unusual situation for her.

And yet the barn door was open and the horse had escaped. There was no rewinding this. She and Wyatt were lovers, and she intended to go wherever it led her.

He stopped on his way to the bed and frowned. "I hate to ask, but should I let that damned cat in?"

She didn't mind that he called Fluffy a damned cat. Because no matter what he said about her kitty, he didn't hate Fluffy. He'd had every reason to after the incident with his bed, but she'd seen him petting Fluffy whenever he twined around Wyatt's legs.

Of course he also called him a little furry bastard. For some silly reason, she was ridiculously amused by that thought.

"Maybe we should."

Wyatt stalked over to the door and opened it. Mr. Fluffypants streaked inside and jumped on the bed. Wyatt headed over and picked up his pants. Disappointment pricked her.

"Are you leaving?"

He glanced at the cat. "I don't trust him around my package, you know?" He grinned. "But that's not enough to make me leave a warm bed with you, Paige."

"Then where are you going?" she asked as he dragged on his pants.

"To fix dinner."

She lay back against the pillows again and stroked Fluffy's soft fur while he purred.

"I could get used to this. Hot sex with a hot man who then fixes me dinner? You're hired for as long as you want."

He frowned and her heart skipped because she knew she'd gone too far.

"Let's get something straight, princess," he said. "I'm your protector because I've been hired to be. But nothing else that happens between us has anything to do with money or jobs. If you think that's the case, then it ends here."

Everybody had a price. She'd learned that early in life. She'd also learned that people only stuck by you when you had something to give them. When there was a benefit for them. But maybe Wyatt was different.

"I'm sorry, Wyatt. I shouldn't have said that. It was a joke, but a bad one."

He scrubbed a hand through his hair. "This is why I didn't want it to get personal. It complicates things when I'm also hired to protect you. Judgments get clouded."

"Are you saying you want to go back to the way it was before?"

"I am saying that. But it's too late, Paige. You're in my blood like a drug. I can't quit you yet."

Yet. Who knew that one word could hurt so much? Because he *would* quit her. It was just a matter of time.

Chapter 19

Wyatt banged around in the kitchen, mad at himself and mad at her too. He shouldn't have given in to the demands of his dick even if it'd been a long time since that particular organ had demanded anything.

He knew better. He was a grown man, and furthermore, he was a damned Navy SEAL. He'd survived BUD/S, for God's sake. Talk about deprivation and pushing your body to its physical limit. He *knew* what it meant to deny himself.

Yet he hadn't denied himself when it came to Paige. He'd sunk into her like a new recruit sank into a hot meal after the first hard day of training. Meaning he'd lost his ever-loving mind.

She'd been soft and sexy and he couldn't say no. He'd wanted her too much.

Hell, his body still suffered aftershocks. Lightning bolts zipped and crashed, and his balls tightened at the thought of sinking into her again.

But first, food.

He found pasta, some sauce in a jar, a package of

hamburger meat, and set about making spaghetti. He wasn't a gourmet cook. Bailey Tucker would be horrified, no doubt, but he could make these things and they tasted good enough to him.

He'd thought Paige was a food snob when they'd gone to No Man's Land for lunch that day, but she'd eaten frozen pizza without complaint. And she'd eaten a lot of staple foods over the past few days, plain stuff that nobody could mistake for gourmet.

But this was the first time he'd really cooked something.

He put the water on to boil, chopped some onion, started it cooking in the pan before adding the meat, and opened the sauce.

Paige emerged from the bedroom. She was wearing yoga pants and a tank top that clung to her breasts. Breasts he'd gotten intimately acquainted with not so long ago. A tingle of arousal began at the base of his spine. He stomped it down.

Her hair was piled on her head in a messy knot. Her smile was uncertain as she came into the kitchen. He wanted to drag her into his arms and kiss her. He resisted the urge, however.

"What are we having?"

"Spaghetti."

"Can I help?"

"Do you know how to boil pasta?"

"I do."

"Then you can do that."

They worked in silence. He wasn't certain whether it was an awkward silence or a companionable one.

"You okay?" he finally asked when the silence was too complete.

She looked up from stirring pasta. "I'm fine."

He wasn't sure he believed her. "Paige."

"I'm okay, Wyatt. Why wouldn't I be?"

"I don't know. But you're quieter than usual."

She shrugged. "I have a lot on my mind. Remember our talk by the river? The videos?" She waved the spoon. "I'm thinking."

He tried not to be bothered that she wasn't thinking about him. Because he was certainly thinking about her. About every kiss and soft moan and touch they'd shared.

Stop.

He grabbed a loaf of frozen garlic bread out of the freezer and turned on the oven. Briefly, he considered sticking his head in the freezer to cool his brain—and other parts of him. Paige would probably think he was nuts if he did.

Wyatt finished up the sauce while she drained the pasta. They fixed bowls, grabbed hot bread fresh from the oven, and put everything on TV trays so they could sit on the couch.

He queued up *American Princess* and Paige groaned. "Do we have to?"

"I'm sorry, Paige, but I need to see. I need to know if there's something being missed in the hunt for this guy."

She sighed. "I know."

He pressed the Play button and settled back to watch. He could tell that Paige was uncomfortable, but he didn't know why. She was magnificent on the screen. Oh, she was rotten to the other women, but they were mostly a bunch of entitled brats anyway. They talked about her. Schemed behind her back. He wondered if one of them could be sending the letters. The voice in them was very male, but that didn't mean a woman couldn't be behind it.

But which one? And why? Didn't make a lot of sense because the threats to Paige focused the attention on her.

Not one of those women wanted that. They wanted the attention on them. If anyone were going to manufacture a stalker, they'd make sure the stalker followed them personally. More attention.

"How's the spaghetti?" Wyatt asked after a few minutes.

Paige glanced over at him. "Take a look."

He peered into her bowl. There were about two bites left. "Guess it was good."

"Delicious. Plus I needed the energy. Have to replace all those calories I lost with you," she said, winking.

Fresh need throbbed to life in his groin. He wanted to go all caveman on her, but he was more civilized than that. For now, anyway.

"I hope you plan to burn a few more tonight. Because I'm not done with you, baby. I can think of a lot more things I'd like to do. You up for that?"

He could see her pulse beating wildly in her throat. "Yes."

Excitement pulsed in his veins, his groin. He'd thought maybe once he had her, it would be enough and he'd go back to that state of disinterest he'd been existing in for the past few months.

Nope. It was like he'd flipped a switch somewhere and all his latent sexual energy came rushing back. Of all the women to arouse that need in him, it had to be the most unattainable one. The one who wasn't from Eagle's Ridge, who wasn't staying, and who existed so far outside his orbit she might as well be from Mars.

He'd watched Ryder, Adam, and Zane fall for women in the past few months and he'd laughed at them. He wasn't falling for Paige, not even close—but even if he'd wanted to, it would have been impossible. She wasn't staying, and he wasn't leaving.

He almost switched off the television and took her back to bed. But something stopped him. Some last shred of professionalism that wouldn't let him neglect watching every episode of her show.

Even if it made him hard to watch her strut across the screen, all that blond hair bouncing and hazel eyes flashing as she dominated the room.

When the episode was over, they put away the food and washed the dishes. Then they settled onto the couch again. Wyatt pulled Paige into the circle of his arm and she sank against his side, her flowery shampoo invading his senses.

He started the next episode as she snaked an arm across his body. She tucked her feet up beneath her and leaned into him. Before long, Fluffy showed up and insisted on climbing across Paige and Wyatt several times.

"Is he going to settle down?" Wyatt asked as the furry bastard kneaded his paws on Wyatt's thigh.

"Pet him. He'll either go away or lie down."

"You know I don't like cats, right?" he said to the animal. Fluffy meowed as if in disbelief.

Paige laughed. "You just don't understand cats. Look how cute he is. And he wants to be on your lap. How is that a bad thing?"

"He also wanted to crap on my bed. That was definitely a bad thing."

She pushed away until she could look up at him. "And a dog wouldn't do something bad? Poop on the floor, eat up your shoe, tear up the furniture?"

She had him there. The last dog he'd had as a kid had chewed the arm right off Gran's sofa one night when they were out shopping. Gran had been furious, and Bear had been relegated to a crate in the laundry room whenever they weren't home. He'd eventually learned not to chew things.

And then there was Gambler, Zane's neurotic dog, who made this cat seem like an angel. A crapping angel, but still.

"Yeah, but a dog wouldn't do it for revenge."

Paige snorted. "You really think Fluffy is that diabolical?"

Wyatt looked into the blue eyes of the cat blinking up at him and knew he was right. "Oh hell yeah."

But he set the remote down and petted the cat's head anyway. Fluffy settled for lying partly on him and partly on Paige. He purred louder than a chainsaw.

"Good boy," Paige murmured.

Wyatt didn't know if she was talking to him or the cat. And then he decided he didn't care. Life was good right now, right here. He was warm, well fed, sexually satisfied, had a beautiful woman beside him and a purring cat on his lap. Well, partially on his lap.

It was domestic. Normal.

He liked it more than he should.

———

PAIGE DOZED. She couldn't help it. Sitting with Wyatt, curled against him, felt good. He was big and warm and she was bored by the show anyway because she'd seen it before. Lived it.

Mr. Fluffypants purred and then fell completely asleep, stretching out until he took up all of Wyatt's lap and hers too. It felt nice to be held and to feel safe. So she slept.

She dreamed off and on about different things, mostly about Wyatt's magic tongue and the way it'd felt when he'd been deep inside her, his big body stroking into hers, driving her toward an orgasm she desperately craved. Everything about being with him had been magical.

A voice burrowed into her subconscious, turning her dream dark and tangled. Instead of Wyatt, it was another man. A man she couldn't see. He held her down, pinned her against the bed, and tried to pry her legs apart so he could shove his way inside her. She screamed.

"Paige. Wake up. Paige."

Her eyes snapped open and Wyatt was there, looking worried and maybe even a little bit angry. Mr. Fluffypants was on the floor, tail switching as if he'd been disturbed in the middle of something.

"I was dreaming," she said, sitting up, blinking.

The room was darkened and the TV was frozen in place because Wyatt had pressed the Stop button.

"You kept saying no, no, no. Then you screamed."

Her heart still hammered and her pulse raced. Tiny beads of sweat popped up on her neck and chest.

"There was a man… It was his voice, Wyatt. It was King's voice. I dreamed about him. He was trying to rape me."

Wyatt pulled her onto his lap and held her close. "It wasn't real, Paige. He's not here."

"It seemed real. I heard him." She laid her head against his shoulder and closed her eyes. "I hate this. I hate that this person has the power to turn my life upside down."

"I know." He stroked her back. "But he won't have that power forever. We're going to catch him, Paige."

She sighed as she put her hand against his cheek and caressed it. "I believe you."

She felt him growing beneath her, his dick swelling and hardening. Arousal soaked her panties. She moved her hips, rubbing her bottom against that delicious hardness.

His eyes flashed with heat and longing. "Careful, sweetheart, or I'll strip you naked and take you on this couch."

"Don't tease me, Wyatt. Just do it."

She needed him to chase away the bad dreams, the terrible feelings. The sense of dread hanging over her.

He looked concerned. "You sure?"

"Yes. Please."

"You got it, baby."

He pulled her tank top off and unsnapped her bra. She shivered in delight as he stripped her, kissing the flesh he revealed.

She thought he might rush this time, but he didn't. He took his time, stripping her slowly, stoking the flames within her. Driving away the bad dreams. By the time he thrust into her body, she was beyond ready.

"You feel so good," he said as he hovered over her, his body deep within hers, anticipation a tangible thing between them.

"So do you."

"I like being with you, Paige."

"I like being with you too."

He started to move and she closed her eyes, gave herself over to the feelings he evoked. He drove away the darkness, the fear, and replaced it with light and happiness. He made her feel things she'd never felt, but she didn't know how real they were. She didn't trust herself, didn't trust what was happening inside her.

Because if she listened to that little voice inside her, it told her that Wyatt was the only one who would ever keep her heart safe. The only one she could trust. But she'd never been right before, so why listen now? Why believe?

"Where are you, Paige?" Wyatt whispered against the shell of her ear. "Stay here. With me."

She wrapped her arms and legs tight around him as pleasure spiraled tighter.

"I'm here."

He skimmed a hand down her side, slipped it beneath her bottom, and lifted her into him, changing the angle just enough that her breath caught—and then she flew.

PAIGE WOKE in the middle of the night, her body sore and spent. But she was sore in a good way. She stretched and reached for the man beside her—

The bed was empty, except for her and Fluffy, who grumbled in his sleep as she disturbed him.

She sat up, straining her ears against the quiet. Wyatt had carried her in here after they'd made love on the couch, and then he'd made love to her again. They'd fallen asleep in each other's arms. But now he was gone.

Her heart skipped. Had he gone back to his own room? Why?

The thought that he might have left her bed hurt. She didn't like it, and she didn't like that it bothered her.

Already getting too close. Wanting too much. What was going to happen when it was time to return to Seattle? Would he come see her there?

She didn't think so. She thought of Mary Beth, of Wyatt's concern for her, and knew he wasn't leaving. He'd left the Navy to return to Eagle's Ridge. For his family, even if his family was one woman.

Except his family wasn't one woman. Family for Wyatt was more than genetics. There were the friends he talked about—Ryder, Adam, Zane, Jack, Noah, and Ford—and the people over at No Man's Land. Even Hildie Fontana, though Paige was certain he wouldn't mind leaving Mrs. Fontana behind from time to time.

He was lucky to have such people in his life. She had family—Daddy and Mother, though Mother lived in Paris now and Daddy was married to Melanie, who monopolized his time. And she had Lily. There were others, but none of them loved her. They used her, just as she used them.

A noise caught her attention. Was that the television? She climbed from bed, utterly naked, and paused for a second before striding for the door. She didn't cover herself. She just walked out into the living room where *American Princess* played on-screen.

Wyatt slouched on the couch, eyes intent on the television.

"Wyatt?"

He turned his head. And then he started when he realized she was naked. She tried not to laugh as he let his hot gaze roam her body.

"Paige—what the hell?"

She abruptly realized the air was chilly and wished she'd grabbed her robe. But, on the other hand, Wyatt's reaction was worth it.

"I was wondering where you went."

He took a blanket off the back of the couch and shook it out. "Come here."

She went over and he pulled her into his lap, covering her. He was only wearing a pair of shorts, so it was easy to feel his burgeoning erection.

Oh, sex on the menu again—did it get any better?

Except he didn't make a move. Instead, he tucked her tight against his chest and hit the button to start the episode again. It was the eighth episode. He'd been up for a while apparently.

Paige laid her cheek on his chest and closed her eyes again. She could sleep like this. Right here in his arms.

Until a voice made her jump out of her skin.

Chapter 20

"That's him," Paige said, bolting up off his lap and pointing at the television. "That's him!"

Wyatt jumped up too, grabbing the remote to pause the show. The man on-screen was shadowed because he wasn't the focus of the scene. Wyatt rewound the program to when he'd first appeared, but he was never in focus.

Paige trembled. She wrapped the blanket tighter over her body and stared at the television. Wyatt put an arm around her to reassure her.

"Who is he, Paige?"

"I… He was my bodyguard. He didn't last very long. He was terrible at the job. The studio hired him for me, and he was on the set a few times. In the background, mostly. Could you play the scene? Please?"

Wyatt pressed Play. The scene continued and the man stayed blurred. But then Paige got up to leave the restaurant where she was lunching with her friend Lily and snapped her fingers at the man.

"Get the car, Joshua."

"Yes, Miss Spencer."

"Oh my God," she said, one hand on her forehead while the other clutched the blanket. "How did I not recognize his voice before?"

"Probably because you were used to hearing it in person. And I'm going to guess you weren't around him a lot."

"No, just for the show. And a few appearances. He lasted about a month—and then at one appearance, a charity ball for cancer patients, a man walked up to me on the red carpet and picked me up in his arms. Joshua didn't see it coming and didn't prevent it. He was fired the next morning. I never saw him again. That was almost two months ago."

"Joshua. Do you know his last name?"

"No. But I can find out."

Wyatt took her by the shoulders and forced her to look at him. "Paige, if I impress nothing else upon you for the rest of your life, let it be this. Don't allow anyone to hire a bodyguard for you. You do it. Interview them, make sure you're comfortable. Know who they are before letting them be in charge of your safety, okay?"

She bit her lip and dropped her gaze. "You're right."

"I know I'm right."

"I didn't hire you though," she pointed out.

"I know that—but you got lucky with me. I know what I'm doing. Besides, your father went to the best firm he could—Hunter Security. It's fine to do that, but always have the final say in your protector, okay?"

"Yes."

He hated the idea of her leaving here, of her having another bodyguard besides him, but that was the reality of their lives. He gathered her in his arms and squeezed her tight.

"You gonna be okay?"

"Yes."

"I need to make some calls."

She tilted her head back. "It's the middle of the night."

He skated a thumb over her cheek. "I know. But people in my business are used to being awakened with this kind of news. It's important to get started on it now. We have to find him and get him in custody."

"I have to call the producer for his last name—"

"No, you don't. I've got it from here. Trust me."

The look she gave him squeezed his heart.

"I do trust you, Wyatt."

"You feel like going back to bed? Or do you want to stay with me while I make calls?"

"I want to stay with you."

"Okay. Sit down and find something else to watch. Or turn the TV off if you want." He handed her the remote. She switched it off without hesitation. He almost grinned. "You still cold?"

"A little."

"Soon as I get my guys working on this, I'll build a fire."

"That would be great. Thanks."

Wyatt grabbed his phone and dialed Hawk's number. The man answered on the second ring.

"Wyatt," he said, his voice scratchy with sleep.

"Hey, man. Sorry to wake you. But Paige has identified her stalker."

"That's great." He could hear Hawk moving around. Getting out of bed maybe. "Give me the details," he said after a few more moments.

"He's a guy the studio hired to work as a bodyguard for her on set and at appearances. He was fired about two months ago. All she knows is his name is Joshua—but the studio should have complete information on him."

"How did she remember all this?"

"I've been watching episodes of *American Princess*. She recognized his voice as the man who called her this morning."

"Damn." In the background, a kid's voice suddenly sounded. Wyatt couldn't tell what was said though. "No, it's okay, buddy," Hawk replied. "Daddy will get the monsters in a minute. Soon as he gets off the phone."

Wyatt couldn't help but grin. Smart kid, asking one of the best snipers HOT had ever had to clear the room of bogeymen.

"Sorry about that," Hawk said a second later. "Monsters. Gotta get 'em."

"Oh yeah, no doubt."

"I'll get this other monster too. Soon as I put the kid back to bed, I'm on the phone, waking the Seattle PD and the studio heads. We'll get this guy."

"Thanks, Hawk."

"I'll let you know when we have the all clear for Miss Spencer to return home."

Something very like a giant stone sank into his belly and refused to move. "Yeah, good. I'm sure she'll be happy to get back."

Paige glanced up at him, eyebrows drawing low as she frowned.

"Thanks, Wyatt. I appreciate everything you've done. Taking this on at the last minute for me—think you might consider doing more jobs for Hunter Security in future?"

"I don't know," he said, as indecision chipped away at his resolve. He *liked* using his skills, even if all he'd done was set up a perimeter and protect a client. "I don't really want to leave Eagle's Ridge very often."

"Let me know if you change your mind."

"Yeah, I will. Thanks."

"Be in touch."

Paige wasn't looking at him when he ended the call. Instead, she was sitting with her knees drawn up and her eyes downcast. Wyatt went over to the fireplace and began building the fire he'd promised. He thought Paige might say something eventually, but she didn't.

After he lit the fire, he turned to her.

"What's on your mind, honey?"

Her lashes lifted and her hot gaze bored into him. "Did he ask you to stay on as my bodyguard?"

"Why do you think that?"

"You said you didn't want to leave Eagle's Ridge very often."

"He asked me if I wanted to work for his firm. You thought I was turning down a job working for you?"

She shrugged. "Maybe."

"I wasn't, Paige. But I still don't want to leave Eagle's Ridge." Not when he'd given up so much to return in the first place. Not when he'd sworn to himself to take care of Gran. Not that she let him do much in that regard, but he was here and she saw him often. Plus he was near if she needed him.

"Oh." Her voice was small. Her lashes dipped again. "When can I go home?"

It was funny how those words struck him. "Not quite yet. Hawk will let us know."

"Will you take me to the airport and wave at me as I walk through the gate?"

She sounded bitter, but he wasn't quite sure if he was hearing her right. It was late and they were both tired.

"I don't know, Paige. I don't know how any of this is going down yet."

She blew out a breath and turned her face to the fire. "I'm sorry. I'm being grumpy. You don't deserve that."

"You've been through a lot."

"Have I? Others go through worse. You went through worse. All that happened to me was some asshole sent me nasty, threatening messages. That's not really a lot in the scheme of things, is it?"

Wyatt went to the kitchen and got a beer. Then he poured a glass of the white wine she liked and brought it back. He was very aware of her nakedness under that blanket, but he wasn't going to take advantage of it.

Yet.

He handed her the glass and sat beside her, taking a swig from the bottle. The flames crackled and the scent of wood filled the air. The cabin glowed warmly. It was summer, but it was cool on the mountain at night.

He pictured this place in winter, with snow as far as the eye could see. There'd be a Christmas tree in the corner, lights blinking cozily, and he and Paige would sit in front of the fire and drink wine before making love on the bearskin rug.

Wyatt shook himself and took another drink. Joshua Whatshisname wasn't caught yet, so he wouldn't get drunk, but the beer sure tasted good.

"Honey, it's not a contest," he finally said.

She stirred beside him. She'd been staring at the fire too.

"Bad is bad. There aren't degrees of bad. This guy upended your life with his threats. He may be a crank, or he may just be angry he lost his job. Either way, his actions affected you. You're allowed to be grumpy."

"Thank you." She sipped her wine. "How did you do it, Wyatt?"

"Do what?"

"Be a SEAL. If everything that's ever been written or

157

filmed about SEALs is to be believed, it's the most dangerous job in the military."

"All special operations are dangerous, no matter the branch of service." He sighed. "But it's what I was trained to do, what I wanted to do. They don't hand you a gun and ship you out on the first day. It takes months of training to be a sailor in the first place. And many months more to be a SEAL. I made it through the first time. Not everyone does that. But I did. I didn't ring the bell."

"Ring the bell?"

"When you can't take it anymore. There's a bell and you go and ring it. No questions asked, you're done. But you aren't coming back and you won't be a SEAL. I didn't ring the bell. I was determined not to."

"Do you miss it?"

"The truth?"

She nodded.

"Every damned day." Because there was something amazing about fighting for your country. About rescuing hostages and taking down terrorists before they could do more harm. The world was filled with bad guys. It was also filled with good people—and they needed people like him and his brothers- and sisters-in-arms.

There *were* still people like him out there, doing the job. That's how he slept at night.

"I'm sorry you had to give it up."

"It's okay. I chose my path."

"You sometimes seem like you wish you'd made a different choice."

He almost couldn't speak because she'd nailed him so perfectly. His friends hadn't even guessed this much. How did she?

He decided to go for brutal honesty. "I couldn't stay. I failed Danny. I won't stay and fail someone else on another mission. And I won't make Gran go through what Lisa and Emma went through. She's never going to sit beside a casket and get a folded flag handed to her by an honor guard."

"I'm sorry, Wyatt." She squeezed his hand, and he squeezed hers back.

"I know, baby. I appreciate it."

Paige looked thoughtful for a moment. "I want to tell you a story."

"Okay."

"When I was sixteen, there was a man who worked for my father. He was about thirty, I think. He was handsome, interesting. I probably flirted with him. It's what I did, what I'd learned. One night, at my father's house, there was a party. He asked me to come with him because he wanted to show me something. I followed him to a room on the second floor, thinking he had something interesting." She fiddled with the edge of the blanket, running it between her fingers. Then she looked at him. "He exposed himself to me. Just shoved his pants down and stood there with his penis waving around and asked me to touch it. To put it in my mouth, in fact."

Fury formed into an iron ball inside him. "Why are you telling me this?"

"Because I blamed myself. I ran, of course. Out of the room and down the stairs, back to the party where I was surrounded by people. I was so scared. I was sixteen. But he was older, and he worked for my father, and I somehow thought it was my fault. That I made it happen. And I was scared everyone would know how awful I was."

"It wasn't your fault," Wyatt growled.

"I know that now. But I didn't then. What I'm saying, Wyatt..." She swallowed and squeezed his hand again. "It's not your fault what happened to your friend. And if you think it is, maybe you should talk to someone about it."

He wanted to shove away from her and go to his room, slam the door. How dare she? But he made himself stay even while his temples throbbed with emotion. She didn't deserve his anger. "I did talk to someone. They make you do that after a mission."

She smiled softly. "Okay then. I just... I remember what you said, that you wished it had been you instead of Danny. And you seem to blame yourself for not saving him, even though you said being a SEAL is the most dangerous job in the world. It was for him too, and he knew it." She hesitated. "I'm glad it wasn't you who died, Wyatt. I'm glad you're here with me."

———

PAIGE COULDN'T QUITE BELIEVE she'd admitted that to him. Then again, what was wrong with it? She hadn't asked him to pick out wedding dates or anything. Surely he couldn't get upset about something so innocuous. And yet she felt as if she'd exposed herself in some way. Left her heart dangling in the breeze.

Which didn't make sense because what did that mean? That she cared about him?

Her mouth went dry. That's *precisely* what it meant.

Oh no. Oh dear heaven, *no*.

He wasn't hers, was never going to be hers. And she wasn't so pitiful as to fall for a man simply because they'd had sex.

It's more than that and you know it.

She wanted to shake her head. To deny it.

But she couldn't. Some crazy part of her was falling for this man.

Wyatt's gaze was stormy, brooding. He closed his eyes. She swallowed. What if he knew how she felt? What if he said he was sorry and looked at her with pity in his eyes?

But he didn't look.

"Thanks," he finally said. He studied their hands where they were still joined, and her heart beat like mad. "I feel less guilty as time goes on, but that bothers me too. Like why is it any better just because it's been a few months? Lisa still doesn't have a husband, and Emma doesn't have a dad."

"Oh, Wyatt." She wanted to hold him, but she didn't dare. Not now when she was so confused. "It's not better. It just hurts a little less, that's all. You won't forget him. They won't either. You just learn how to live without him."

"You sound like you have experience," he said, frowning.

"Lily—that's Lily Ashwood, from the show—had a younger sister. She was born with a congenital heart defect. She died when she was ten and we were fifteen. It was hard on Lily and her family. I was there. I hurt too, but nothing like they did."

"You two are close?"

Paige found herself hesitating. "We were. I think maybe we've grown apart a bit. She'll always be my bestie. But I think we want different things out of life. I feel like we're moving in different directions."

Lily wanted to fly to Paris and buy expensive handbags. Paige wanted to make videos about her ideas and gain viewers so she could entice a business partner to work with her. Lily would always be content being an Ashwood and living off her parents' money. She'd marry someone eventually, but it would be the *right* someone. Someone with a fortune equal to hers.

Paige wasn't sure that mattered. In fact, she was certain

it didn't. It wasn't what a man had that mattered. It was what he could give you. And by that she meant the intangible things he could give you. Love, belonging, happiness.

"Don't let that relationship go, Paige. Not if it means anything to you. People grow apart, but I've had the same best friends since I was in high school. We all got detention together for a semester, and we've been friends since. I could call any of them up and they'd drop everything to help me. I'd do the same for them."

"What do they say about what happened with Danny?"

He frowned. "I didn't tell them."

"Why not? You said they're your best friends. Why wouldn't you tell them?"

And yet he'd told her. It wasn't lost on her that she knew something about him that his friends didn't.

"I didn't want to bring them down. They've all had their own things going on, and I've only just come back to town. It's not fair to burden them with my problems when they've got lives of their own."

She couldn't believe what she was hearing. "Wyatt, for God's sake—that's what they're for. Your friends want to help you. If they've been your best friends since high school, then I'm sure they care about you. Do you at least talk to them regularly?"

"Just about every day. Well, Ryder, Zane, and Adam anyway. They live in Eagle's Ridge. Jack lives in Seattle, and Ford lives in Virginia Beach. Noah's in DC, but he's coming back soon. His cousin is dying. He's taking custody of her little daughter, Bella."

Paige couldn't help but put a hand over her heart in sympathy. "Oh no."

"Yeah, it's pretty tragic. Lainey is a sweetheart. And Bella—" He sighed. "Well, she's a doll. I've babysat her a couple of times. Bright kid. She's going to be okay with Noah, but she's going to have it rough too."

"Of course she will. Losing a mother can't be easy."

The fire crackled and popped, and he reached for the edge of the blanket, parting it to reveal her naked body. Goose bumps rose on her skin. Her breath caught and her sex ached.

"I'm tired of talking about sad things," Wyatt said. "I'd rather do something happy."

She lay back and spread her legs so he could see everything. "Does this make you happy?"

He slipped a finger into her folds, stroked over her clit while she bit the inside of her lip and tried not to sound too needy.

"It's a good start."

Chapter 21

Paige was happy. Deliriously happy. And she shouldn't be. Not really. She had work to do, a life to get back to.

But every moment with Wyatt Chandler carved another notch into her heart. She lay in his arms, on the bear rug in front of the fireplace, and didn't care that it was a cliché.

Bear rugs and lovemaking went perfectly together. No wonder it was a fantasy. Her body still tingled from the aftermath, her mind going back over everything they'd said to each other tonight.

They'd said a lot, much of it about feelings—but none of it about feelings that had to do with each other. She thought of returning to Seattle soon and her chest began to ache. What would she do when she didn't have this?

Her eyes teared up as she listened to Wyatt breathing. He was asleep, his chest rising and falling evenly. She wanted to look at him, but that would mean turning in his arms and disturbing him. She wouldn't do that because he needed sleep.

She couldn't sleep though. She'd been thinking about

everything that had happened over the past twenty-four hours. Her relationship with Wyatt had moved onto a new level—but what did it mean to him? Anything?

Probably not. She had to acknowledge that fact and face it head-on.

She also had to face whatever happened with her stalker. What happened when they caught him? Would there be a trial?

She tried to remember everything she could about Joshua, but the truth was she'd hardly paid him any attention. He'd been like a prop to her, soon forgotten once he was gone. He'd been average height. Bigger build than average. Good-looking but not memorably so. He'd never gone home with her, but that wasn't because the studio hadn't wanted him to.

She hadn't wanted him to. She'd insisted she didn't need personal security in her home. She lived in a building with its own security, and she'd felt perfectly safe there. But Joshua had dropped her at her building. And he knew which apartment she lived in.

He knew because he buzzed up to her once, when she was running late and not answering her phone—she'd accidentally turned off the ringer—in order to tell her he was outside with a car.

My God, that man had driven her places. Been by her side for a month on set and at appearances. It made her shiver. He could have done something to her then. He could have taken her somewhere and raped her or held her for ransom. He could have killed her.

She lay in Wyatt's arms for another hour, letting her thoughts drive her crazy. The fire banked and glowed. The sun began to rise over the valley. The darkness in the room grew lighter as the sun slipped into the sky.

"Ready for coffee?" Wyatt growled into her ear.

She jumped, tingled, and melted all at once. "Yes. How did you know I was awake?"

"I felt it in the tension of your body."

"I didn't want to wake you."

"You didn't. I wake early. I also sleep in snatches. Learned that on patrol." He ran his fingers down her side beneath the blanket they lay under. "How long have you been awake?"

"A while. I couldn't stop thinking about things."

"Joshua?"

"Yes." She pulled in a breath. "He was close to me for a month. He could have done anything."

"But he didn't. You have to remember that. He didn't."

"I know. It's just so… creepy."

"Yeah, I know. But he's not getting near you again, Paige. I won't let it happen."

He got to his feet and pulled her up, wrapping the blanket around her and kissing her forehead. Then he grabbed his athletic shorts from where they'd landed on the chair and slipped them on before going over and fixing the coffeepot.

A shaft of sunlight came through the window, illuminating his body, and she watched him with a troubled heart. He meant something to her. More than she wanted him to.

She'd never been in love before—didn't think she was now—but how did anyone ever know? Was it a lightning bolt? A spreading warmth like sinking into a hot bath?

"You want breakfast now or later?"

She shook herself. "Definitely now. I'm starved."

He looked up and grinned, and her heart careened out of control. "Me too. You gave me a workout."

"I gave *you* a workout? That last time wasn't my idea, mister."

"Yeah, but did you mind?"

"Not at all."

"I didn't think so." He opened the refrigerator. "Eggs and bacon with toast?"

"Sounds good to me." What was wrong with her? Back in Seattle, she'd be having a protein smoothie. Organic, of course. But here, with Wyatt, she thought bacon and eggs sounded like the perfect meal to start the day.

What the hell. Enjoy it while you can.

"Coming right up."

"Need help?"

"No, I got this. You can wash the dishes."

She didn't even bat an eye at doing a task she rarely ever did when at home. "Sounds like a plan."

"Only one condition," Wyatt said.

"What?"

"You have to do it naked."

⸺

AFTER BREAKFAST and conversation that managed to avoid any sensitive topics, they went their separate ways to shower and dress. When Paige got back to the living room, Wyatt was sitting at the dining room table, staring at his computer screen. He looked up and smiled, and her breath tripped and fell inside her chest. Took it a moment to regain its feet too.

"You want to go into town today? Maybe have lunch at that fancy new restaurant Bailey Tucker opened?"

"That sounds lovely. Can we invite Mary Beth?"

He looked pleased at the suggestion. "Sure. But you have to promise to help me discourage her from ordering dessert."

"I'll do my best."

He shook his head. "Guess that's the most any of us can hope for."

Paige worked on her ideas until it was time to go, writing out lists of things she'd need to do her videos, planning how to stage the outfits, how best to set everything up. It wasn't that it hadn't been done before. *What Not to Wear* and *How Do I Look?* were two of her favorites. But those shows took someone on a shopping spree rather than taking them into stores and showing them how to buy for themselves on a regular basis.

Paige's idea was to set up the shopping trips using what she could find in the store and then introducing her own clothing ideas as well. It wasn't as grand as she'd imagined in the first place, but it was forward motion. And she was excited about it, which was fun.

Around ten, they went out to the truck and started down the mountain. Wyatt had set his alarms as if he still expected trouble. It bothered her more than she liked. They knew who they were looking for now, but until they had Joshua, he could be anywhere.

Even Eagle's Ridge.

For some reason, knowing who he was made it worse. Especially because he'd been near her for a solid month and she hadn't known he was nuts. Or inclined to be nuts.

Once they reached Eagle's Ridge, Wyatt parked near the square again, and they got out to explore until it was time for their lunch reservation at Blue Moon. Wyatt had offered to pick Mary Beth up, but in her typically independent fashion, she'd said she would meet them there.

The shops were cute, quaint, and Paige discovered that even if they weren't filled with the latest designer fashions, she rather enjoyed browsing through them. There were local goods—jams, jellies, crafts, and even wine—in some of them. There was a small clothing boutique she hadn't seen earlier, and she made a beeline for it.

Wyatt managed to reach the door before she did and held it open so she could walk inside. The shop was long and narrow, but the floors were wide-plank walnut and the walls were aged brick. There were clothing racks, but most of them held T-shirts with pithy sayings. There were some leggings, a few lace tops, and a shelf of scarves on one wall.

There was also some lingerie with naughty sayings and feathers. Almost like it was joke lingerie, though Paige suspected it wasn't.

The selection was disappointing. Paige frowned as she strolled through the store. A young woman emerged from the back stock room.

"Hi. Can I help you find anything?"

"Just browsing," Paige said.

"Hey, Wyatt," the woman said, her gaze sliding past Paige to land on the man behind her.

And just like that, Paige's hackles rose. A prickling sensation flowed through her veins, leaving behind goose bumps on her skin. She grew hot.

Jealousy? Really?

"Hey, Claudia," he said. "How're you doing?"

"Good. Haven't seen you since that night at Baldie's a couple of weeks back."

"Yeah, I've been busy."

The woman's gaze flicked to Paige again. "You must be Nicole." She cocked her head. "You look familiar though."

"I get that a lot," Paige said, smiling.

Claudia snapped her fingers. "Wait a minute—Paige Spencer! From *American Princess*, am I right?"

Paige met Wyatt's eyes. They were hard but resigned.

"That's right," Wyatt said. "But Paige is here incognito.

We'd appreciate it if you don't mention it to anyone else in town."

Claudia shrugged. "Who would I tell? I know probably three other people who watch the show besides me."

Paige tried not to let that statement sting. Didn't work.

"I guess we aren't that popular," she said with a smile, walking over and shaking the woman's hand. "Probably why they put us on hiatus."

"I think you were finding your groove—but the problem is there are already too many shows with catty women behaving badly. Yours is just another competing to be heard in all the noise." Claudia's eyes widened. "Oh, wait. I'm sorry I said that. Catty, I mean. I'm sure you really aren't."

Paige wasn't sure the woman was sincere at first, but her cheeks reddened and Paige knew she wasn't faking it. She really was worried she'd offended.

"It's okay. I knew what I was getting into when I vamped it up on the show. You can say it. I'm a total bitch."

Claudia laughed. "Well, yeah. But it's television, right?"

"I hope so. Though Wyatt might have a different opinion."

Claudia's gaze went to Wyatt again. If Paige wasn't mistaken, there was a hint of dreaminess to the look she gave him. Jealousy reared its ugly head again.

"How do you know Paige, Wyatt?"

"Her dad owns a house here. I'm the hired protection."

"Ah, of course. Using the military training."

"Yep."

"That's not what Hildie Fontana thinks."

"Never is."

Claudia laughed. "You are so right."

The bell on the door tinkled again, and a gorgeous redhead walked in. She was a little older but absolutely stunning. Paige caught sight of Wyatt and noted that his jaw had gone a little slack.

"Miss Wood," Claudia said, rushing over to the redhead. "What can I help you with today?"

"I'm just looking for something for a friend."

Miss Wood's gaze floated over to Paige and Wyatt standing there. She smiled as she walked over.

"Hello, Wyatt. How are you?"

"Miss Wood—" He cleared his throat as if he'd been about to say something else. "Uh, fine Miss Wood. How are you?"

Even her voice was sexy. Sensual. Like a real-life Jessica Rabbit.

"Wonderful." Her gaze slid over to Paige.

"This is Nicole, Miss Wood," Wyatt said.

Miss Wood arched an elegant eyebrow. "Don't lie, Wyatt. This is Paige Spencer from *American Princess*. I'm pleased to meet you. And you can call me Diana."

Paige shook the woman's hand.

Claudia clapped and squealed. "Oh em *gee*, do you watch it too?" she exclaimed. "That's so cool!"

Diana smiled. Everything about the woman was elegant. "It's a guilty pleasure. I also like *The Real Housewives of Orange County*. Well, all the housewife shows if I'm honest."

Wyatt looked like he'd been slapped over the skull with a two-by-four. He shook his head and backed away. "I'm going to stand outside. You ladies continue." He gave Paige a significant look. She acknowledged it with a smile.

He disappeared through the door, bell tinkling, and took up a fighting stance outside. So serious and sexy, that man. She wanted to jump him and kiss the daylights out of him.

Diana and Claudia turned their gazes on Paige. She hoped what she'd been thinking hadn't shown.

"He's her bodyguard," Claudia said. "It's hush-hush."

"Yes, I'd heard he had a girlfriend in town. From Virginia, I think."

"That's just my cover," Paige said. "I didn't want anyone to know I was here. Please don't share it."

"Wouldn't dream of it. But don't tell Hildie Fontana or the whole world will know," Diana said with a laugh.

"Oh God," Claudia chimed in. "I love her, but she sure can tell some tall tales."

"Yes, she really can. But she means well in her own way."

"How long have you had this store?" Paige asked, wanting to turn the attention away from her and her secrets.

"About a year." Claudia frowned. "It's been tough though."

"Why?"

She waved a hand at the T-shirts. "I'd like to put in some quality merchandise, but everyone wants this stuff. I have to carry it, or I sell nothing at all."

Paige's senses prickled. She turned her eye on the store, envisioning displays of clothing and accessories. Upscale decor with budget pricing. Dressing rooms with soft lighting that flattered and enhanced. Maybe a coffee and champagne bar too. Upbeat music, but not too loud or boisterous.

But this wasn't her town, and she wasn't staying. Still, the ideas excited her.

"I have some ideas if you want them," Paige said.

Claudia's eyes widened. "Oh, well, that's nice of you.

But I can't afford to stock Jimmy Choo or Versace. A single Louis Vuitton would break the bank for months."

"No, nothing like that. But really, fashion is my thing. I know a bit about it. If you ever want to talk." She fished a card from her purse, one of the ones she'd had made for the executives she'd been meeting with. "Call me if you want to hear my ideas."

Claudia turned the card in her fingers. "I'll do that. Thank you."

She wasn't certain the other woman would, but at least she'd tried. "Well, I'd better get going. We have lunch reservations."

Diana Wood lit up. "Blue Moon?"

"Yes. How did you know?"

"It's the only place in town you need a reservation. But it's *so* worth it. Very French. Very delicious. It was lovely to meet you, Paige."

"You too." Paige waved at the women as she walked out the door. Wyatt pushed away from the wall where he'd been waiting, his gaze heating as it passed over her. She liked it, and she'd liked imagining the shop done up right too.

"You done in there?"

"Yep." As they walked away, she snorted as she remembered the way he'd looked at Diana Wood. It hadn't made her jealous, though maybe it should have. Except it was too funny. Like he'd had a childhood crush or something. "Want to tell me what that was with Diana?"

"Oh hell, you noticed that?"

"I think we all did, Wyatt."

"Shit. I'm leaving town then. First thing tomorrow."

She playfully punched his arm. "You aren't and you know it."

"No, not really." He sighed. "Miss Woody—and yeah, I

nearly said that—was the object of a million teenage fantasies. Remember those best friends I mentioned?"

"Yes."

"She was the detention monitor that semester. We spent a lot of time thinking about her. And we called her Miss Woody for obvious reasons."

Paige laughed. "Poor woman. The source of a thousand teenage erections."

"Millions, probably. Can't figure out why she never married, though I have to admit we all thought we had a chance once we were older. Figured one of us would marry her. Didn't happen though."

"She's gorgeous."

"She definitely is. But so are you." He turned and caught her to him when they passed behind a hedge in Sentinel Park. "She made me hot when I was sixteen. You make me hot now."

Paige melted into his arms for a leisurely kiss that had them both breathing a bit heavier.

"Oh my!"

Wyatt stiffened and they broke apart. Hildie Fontana stood there in another of her colorful caftans, silver hair gleaming in the sun filtering through the trees. In her hands she had a bag from the bakery and a coffee.

"Morning, Mrs. Fontana," Wyatt said.

Paige tried not to laugh. She really did. But this woman seemed to catch them every single time he kissed her in town. It was like he had a magnet on him that drew her the instant his lips touched Paige's. She couldn't stop the laughter that burst from her.

Hildie wasn't deterred. "Morning, Wyatt. Morning, Nicole. Are you two ever coming to the shop or what?"

"I would love to," Paige said, still giggling from time to time. "Wyatt?"

He looked like he'd rather wrestle a bear. "Sure. Yeah."

"I'm sorry, Mrs. Fontana. I'm just so happy. I can't stop laughing."

"Oh honey, of course you are," Hildie said. "With a man like Wyatt in your corner, life is very rosy."

Paige shot him a look. "Yes, ma'am, it definitely is. Wyatt? You ready to go have a look around Mrs. Fontana's shop?"

"Yeah. You bet."

Paige curled her arm in his and they followed a chattering Hildie all the way across the square and back to her cute little antique shop.

But by the time they got there, Paige's spirits had dampened. She'd been having fun, but it wouldn't last. Soon she'd be on her way back to Seattle. And Wyatt wasn't going with her.

Chapter 22

Lunch at Blue Moon with Gran and Paige was a very bad idea. Wyatt nursed his glass of water and watched the two of them. Gran liked her, it was clear. And Paige liked Gran.

They laughed and talked about horses, about coffee, about baking the perfect coffee cake. They exclaimed over the food too. Bailey came over and talked to them for a few minutes, blushing a little at all the compliments over her cuisine. She really was a fine chef. Wyatt had known her since they were kids, back when she'd just been Adam and Zane's annoying baby sister, but she'd certainly come into her own. Dating Ryder and everything.

"Are you ready for dessert?" she asked them.

"Yes," Paige and Gran said at the same time that Wyatt said, "No."

He glared at Paige. Gran rolled her eyes.

"Bailey, dear," she said, "do you have something that's sugar free?"

Wyatt relaxed, but only marginally.

"I have a sugar-free chocolate torte. We serve it with

whipped cream and fresh strawberries. Believe me, you won't even know the difference."

"Then I'll have that," Gran said. "And a coffee."

"Make that two," Paige added.

Wyatt let out a long-suffering sigh. "Fine. Three."

"Excellent. I'll let your server know."

"Wyatt William, you sure are grumpy today," Gran said after Bailey was gone. "What's the matter with you?"

"Nothing, Gran. I'm not grumpy at all."

Paige smirked. When they got back to the cabin, he was going to spank her. And then he was going to lick her.

"Hildie caught us in the park and forced us to go over to her shop," Paige said, eyeing him. "She's been asking and Wyatt's been promising, but this time he couldn't think up an excuse."

"Oh my," Gran said.

"We spent half an hour looking at estate jewelry while she whipped out ring after ring and pronounced them good engagement rings. Or, at the very least, promise rings."

Gran laughed. "Hildie is a force to be reckoned with. Did you buy anything?"

Paige dropped her lashes, and Wyatt suddenly felt uncomfortable. Why the hell had he insisted on buying her anything anyway?

"Wyatt bought me a pin." She dug the velvet box from her purse and handed it over. The cat was as pretty now as it had been in the shop. Silver, with green jewels for eyes, it was a lovely little thing. And perfect for Paige.

Gran studied it. When she looked up at Wyatt, he thought he couldn't possibly get any more uncomfortable than he was right that minute. He could see the spark of hope in her eyes, the wish that he might settle down and start having grandchildren. He hated to disappoint her—because that's not what was happening here.

He liked Paige. But what they had was physical, not lasting. He loved her body, not her. Loved the way he felt when he was buried inside her—but he would feel that way with any woman.

It was sex. The euphoria of sex. That wasn't love and never would be.

"She has a cat," Wyatt said gruffly. "It seemed appropriate."

Paige had tried to tell him no, especially since the pin had been nearly two hundred dollars. But he'd talked Hildie down and bought it anyway. He could afford to spend that much, even if Paige was accustomed to spending far more.

He'd wanted to get her the pin, but he felt stupid now. She'd been nice about it, but she could afford anything she wanted. Hell, her watch was Cartier. The diamonds in her ears could choke a horse. But she'd gazed up at him with tears in her eyes when he'd bought that pin.

Even now, she treated it like it was precious.

"I love it," she said. "It's perfect."

Gran shifted her gaze to Paige. Then she patted Paige's hand. "It is, honey. You're a sweet girl."

Wyatt stifled an inner groan. This had been a spectacularly bad idea. He'd just been trying to take care of Gran, protect Paige, and have a nice lunch. Instead, he'd gotten up the hopes of one, made a fool of himself with the other, and the day wasn't even over yet.

The cake and coffee arrived then, and he was saved from continuing the conversation. He had to admit, after the first hesitant bite, that the cake was pretty damned amazing. Ryder was going to weigh three hundred pounds in about ten years with Bailey's cooking.

But what a way to go.

"Will you two be going to the Fourth of July festivities?" Gran asked.

"Paige might be back in Seattle by then," Wyatt said before Paige could answer.

"I don't know yet," Paige blurted. "Nothing is settled. But I might have to go."

Gran's gaze darted between them. "Have you found her stalker?"

"He's been identified. But he's not in custody yet," Wyatt told her.

"Well, I hope he gets caught soon. And I also hope you stay for the fun, dear," Gran said. "Eagle's Ridge really does it right."

"I'd like to," Paige said, but Wyatt didn't think she meant it. She was a city girl at heart, and she wanted to get back there. Besides, she had her plan now, and he didn't think anything was going to stop her. Paige Spencer was going to be a success on her own terms, no doubt about it.

Yet part of him wished she was a small-town girl. That her dreams weren't so big and that she might want to stay in Eagle's Ridge and spend the winter cozied up in a firelit cabin with him.

"It's only a couple of days away now. Maybe you'll still be here," Gran said with a smile.

"Yes, maybe so."

"Don't get your hopes up. Either of you," Wyatt said. "This has always been a job—and once it's over, Paige is going home. And I'm moving on."

"Of course, dear," Gran said, looking slightly scandalized. Maybe he had been a bit blunt.

Paige didn't respond. Or look at him. She forked up a bite of her cake and kept her attention anywhere but on him.

Wyatt ignored the sinking feeling in his gut. *It's a job*, he told himself. *A job.*

But sometimes it felt like a lot more.

His phone buzzed in his pocket. He took it out and glanced at it. Turning away from his lunch companions, he took the call.

"They got him," Hawk said. "Joshua Kingsley is in custody."

———

"KINGSLEY," Paige said. She kept turning the name over in her head. How had she not remembered that? He'd called himself King. And he'd called her "my queen." It should have been obvious, but she hadn't remembered a thing about the man who'd spent a month as her part-time protector.

They were back at the cabin and Wyatt was at his computer while she paced back and forth in the living room. She'd put Mr. Fluffypants in her room and shut the door so she could open the french doors onto the deck. The breeze on the mountain was fresh and sweet, though it had been hotter in town. She strode outside and gazed at the valley below.

The sight tugged at her heart. But then she remembered Wyatt's words at lunch. She'd be leaving and he'd be moving on. That's what he'd said. Of course it was the truth, and yet hearing it made a knot form in her chest.

But what had she expected?

He'd bought her the pin, though she'd objected because of the expense, but he'd insisted it hadn't meant anything beyond the moment. Maybe he'd done it to shut Hildie up. Maybe he'd just been being nice.

Wyatt looked up, his expression fierce. "The studio

should have never hired him. He had no experience. He'd once been in the Army for two years, but as a regular grunt. He had no Special Forces training. Nothing to recommend him for the job."

It didn't surprise her, though it did make her angry. The producers were always trying to cut corners. Yes, they were a small production set in Seattle, not a big Hollywood operation. But a security professional should have qualifications, not a vague résumé with some military service.

Huh, maybe she had learned something from Wyatt.

His phone rang and she stopped pacing while he took the call. After a few minutes, he hung up and met her gaze. Her heartbeat slowed. She didn't like that look on his face.

"Your lawyer is filing a temporary restraining order against him. They'll let him go and schedule a court date for a hearing. The judge can grant the order then, or not. It will probably be granted, based on his behavior. The cryptic notes, the photo. The threat against you and your cat. They're vague, but should be enough for a judge."

Paige's heart hammered. "What are you telling me? That he's going to be let go? That he'll be free to keep harassing me?"

He came over and took her by the shoulders. "He won't be free to harass you. If he does, he'll go to jail. But the justice system doesn't lock people up for vague threats, Paige. And that's all he's done. He's entitled to due process."

Anger swirled inside her. "And what about me? What am I entitled to? What am I supposed to do when he knows where I live?"

"You don't have to go back yet. Or, when you do, stay with your father for a while."

Acid scalded her throat. Stay with her father and Melanie? She'd rather spend the night in a snake-filled pit.

"It's not fair," she said. "He's turned my life upside down, and the only assurance I have that he'll quit is a restraining order?"

"I'm afraid so."

She pulled in a breath. "Come to Seattle with me, Wyatt. Protect me there. At least until we're sure he won't violate the order."

His gaze was troubled. His fingers dug into her shoulders. "I can't, Paige. But I'll make sure you have someone good. Hawk runs a high-end firm with former military guys. You'll be safe with his crew."

Her heart hurt. The idea of going back to Seattle no longer appealed. Not without him. It hit her, quite forcefully, that she needed him. That her life wouldn't be the same without him.

Oh my God—was this love? Did she love him?

Oh wow, she did. Loved his grandma too—and loved this mountain and the view. How could she love these things in so little time? And how could he contemplate sending her away so easily? Did he really feel nothing? He'd bought her the silver cat, told her his secrets. Didn't that mean anything?

"I want *you*," she said, her voice quivering.

His fingers tightened on her shoulders. "I can't, honey. I swore I'd be here for Gran. That I'd take care of her. I can't go."

Paige sniffed. "Mary Beth doesn't need taking care of, Wyatt. She needs your love, but she doesn't need you hovering over her like a prison warden."

His brows drew down. "Don't tell me what my grandmother needs. You don't know her at all. A few days in Eagle's Ridge doesn't make you an expert on either one of us."

Oh, he knew how to twist the knife, didn't he? She

pushed out of his grip and went out onto the deck. The breeze fluttered her hair. The tears pricking her eyes grew cool in the wind.

She knew, didn't she, that people only did things for you when you paid them to? That her worth was directly tied to the compensation she could provide. And here she'd fallen for the one man who couldn't be compensated enough to stay by her side.

She heard him come outside. He walked up behind her, his powerful body giving off a lot of heat as he stood close enough to touch. But she refused to turn.

He wrapped his arms around her, bent his head to her ear. "I'm sorry. That was uncalled for."

She wanted to stand firm, not touch him. Not melt. But she wasn't that strong. She put her hands on his arms, held him to her. His lips feathered along her neck, and chills ran up her spine on spidery feet.

"You'll be safe, Paige. I won't let anyone hurt you. I promise."

Except he'd already broken that promise. Because he was the one hurting her—and he didn't even know it.

Chapter 23

In some respects, it was an awkward couple of days. Wyatt and Paige had an unspoken truce going. They didn't talk about the future, though they made love like there wasn't one. He didn't know why it hurt every time they were in bed together, but it did. Hurt right in the center of his chest and wouldn't stop.

In fact, it hadn't stopped hurting since the moment it started two days ago. He could forget it for a short while, and then it came roaring back.

Maybe it was because the temporary restraining order against Joshua Kingsley had been granted and a hearing date set. Which meant that Paige could return to Seattle at any moment. But Hawk didn't have anyone to take over her protection there just yet. It was a holiday weekend and his people were otherwise engaged.

So she was still here, and he was still taking her to bed every night and losing himself in her. If he could just stop doing that, the ache would get better.

But he couldn't. Damn him, but he couldn't.

Since Hawk was shorthanded, Wyatt had been thinking hard about how he could make a difference in that regard, at least in Washington State. Paige was right that he could do something here. He knew plenty of former Special Forces guys. Some of them might like to put their skills to use. Eagle's Ridge was getting more popular as a tourist destination, and there was also the surrounding area to consider. Executives from Seattle had vacation homes here. They often brought their own protection, but what if they could hire a local firm?

It wasn't what he'd thought he might do, but the more he considered it, the more feasible it seemed. He might explore the possibility after Paige was gone.

Paige.

She'd made him think about going to Seattle, but he'd shoved the idea way. It wasn't in his plans, and he resented that she'd even planted the seed. But he'd still thought about it. Hell, he couldn't stop thinking about it. Today was July Fourth, but tomorrow was the fifth, and that meant Hawk would probably have someone available quite soon.

As if thinking it made it happen, his phone rang. It was Hawk.

"I've got someone who can take over tomorrow," he said. "Greg Spencer will send a company plane for her. Her new guard will be onboard."

Wyatt rubbed his chest. "That's good. Who is he?"

"Former Ranger. Name is Eric Reynolds. I'll send over details of the exchange."

"Yeah, sounds good."

"You think any more about coming to work for me? We could use someone with your skills."

Wyatt frowned. "Actually, I was thinking about opening my own protection firm. Right here in Eagle's Ridge. We get enough traffic during the high season to make it worthwhile."

"That sounds like a good idea. Let me know if you need anything. I'd be happy to help—and happy to send clients your way too."

"I appreciate that. I'll let you know if I go through with it."

Paige emerged from her room. Her phone was in her hand.

"I'm going home tomorrow," she said.

"I know."

Her eyes seemed to sparkle. "Ah, okay. Didn't realize you knew."

"Hawk just called."

"I just spoke to Daddy. He's sending a plane—and a new bodyguard."

"Yeah."

They stood there staring at each other. He didn't know what to say, but he felt like he needed to say something. Like if he didn't, he'd burst with the effort of holding it in.

Before he could manage to find the words, his phone rang again. He answered with a clipped, "Yeah."

"Wyatt William Chandler, is that any way to greet your grandmother?"

"Sorry, Gran." Paige was still staring at him. He couldn't take his eyes off her either. Finally he forced himself to turn away. "What's up?"

"Today is the big day. Fireworks, the parade, and I've heard *nothing* from you yet. Are you even coming to the celebration? Hildie needs your opinion about the Navy float."

Wyatt rolled his eyes. "Gran, half the town is former Navy. She can ask one of them. She doesn't need me."

"You are the most recent Navy person to return to

town and it has to be you. She needs to know what you think."

"You're messing with me, Gran."

"I'm not. But even still, you haven't been in town for the Fourth for twelve years, not since you went off to the Navy. You need to be here. You're one of our veterans, and we want to honor you. All your friends will be here."

Wyatt closed his eyes. Hell, maybe it was a good idea. Take Paige to the park, forget about the fact she was leaving tomorrow. Part of him wanted to strip her naked and spend the next twenty-four hours in bed with her, but the other part—the logical part—said that going to the celebration was the best, most distracting thing to do.

Time to move on with life, right? Because nothing was changing about the situation. She had her life in Seattle. His was here. What they had going on wasn't serious enough to warrant him asking her to stay. It was sex.

"I'll be there."

"Excellent. I'll tell Hildie. I'm going to assume you're bringing Paige."

"Yes."

"So can we call her Paige now or is it still Nicole?"

"Whatever she's comfortable with."

Gran huffed. "You are very curt today, young man."

Wyatt rubbed a hand over his forehead. "I don't mean to be. Just have a lot on my mind."

"If you ask me, you need to quit being stubborn and see what's right in front of your face. I have eyes, Wyatt. I can see. You and Paige are crazy for each other—"

"We aren't."

"Don't you interrupt me, Wyatt William."

"Yes, ma'am."

"I know you've only known her for couple of weeks, but there's something there. When I met your grandfather, he swept me off my feet. I knew he was the one from the very first. Even though he was fifteen years older than me, it didn't matter. He was the one. And we were married within a month."

"Gran." She was beginning to sound upset. He didn't like it.

"I'm just saying. Don't be so hidebound you can't see what's in front of your eyes. You've been through a lot the past few months, and you're carrying around something that you won't share with me. But you can't take your eyes off her, honey. I think she means something to you. And I think you're fighting it."

"I'm not fighting anything."

She sighed. "Fine. I tried. When will you be here? I need to tell Hildie."

"Give me an hour."

"Wonderful. And Wyatt?"

"Yes, Gran?"

"I love you. I want you to be happy."

"I love you too."

Paige was sitting on the arm of the couch when he turned around again.

"Everything okay?" she asked.

He shoved his phone in his pocket. "Yeah. Gran wants us to come to the celebration. And Hildie apparently needs my opinion on a float."

Paige smirked. "I didn't know you were an expert on floats, Wyatt."

"I'm a man of many talents," he said wryly.

She smiled, but there was a hint of sadness to it. "I can attest to that. So, when do we go?"

"You don't mind?"

"Of course not. Everyone's been telling me the fireworks and parade are not to be missed. And since it's my last day in Eagle's Ridge..." Her gaze dropped. She nibbled her bottom lip. His groin began to ache.

"You can come back. Come visit us. Gran would love to see you."

Her eyes blazed as she lifted her head. "And you? Would you love to see me too?"

"I would."

"Until you wouldn't."

"What's that supposed to mean?"

She shook her head. "Girlfriends, Wyatt. There'll be one eventually."

His gut churned. "Look, I don't want to talk about this. Let's just go to the celebration and try to have a good time."

"You never want to talk about it. About anything. Did you ever think that maybe you need to stop avoiding the things that bother you and face them head-on?"

"I've spent the past twelve years of my life facing things you can't imagine. I think I'm good."

She got to her feet. "Oh yes, play the Navy SEAL card. Of course you've seen terrible things. But that doesn't mean you get to use that as an excuse to avoid the important things in your life."

"Maybe this isn't all that important. Did you ever think of that?"

The look on her face made him feel like shit. He wanted to call the words back, but it was too late. They'd done their damage. She turned away and went to pick up her purse. She stopped and petted her cat, bent down and kissed his head, then straightened and faced Wyatt with pale cheeks.

"I'm ready when you are."

Say something. Apologize.

189

But maybe it was best if she was angry with him. It'd be easier on them both if they just made a clean break.

———

EAGLE'S RIDGE was decked out for the Fourth. The bunting was everywhere. Sentinel Park was alive with laughing children and adults enjoying the carnival rides and eating things like fried Twinkies on a stick and funnel cakes.

Paige avoided those foods, though she did go for some messy ribs with corn on the cob and coleslaw. The parade was fun too. Kids and adults alike cheered for the floats, the bands, the horses and riders with their flags. Mary Beth rode her horse down Main Street with the other equestrians, waving like a princess.

Paige laughed and waved back. Wyatt waved too, though she could feel the tension in him as his grandmother went by on a twelve-hundred-pound animal subject to spooking from any number of surprises coming at him from all directions.

But the horses in the parade were calm, and the procession kept on going. The Navy float sailed by, a gray ship with sailors on its deck. Hildie had tried to talk Wyatt into riding the float, but he'd refused. She'd eventually accepted his reasoning that he had to stay with Paige.

Everyone knew her real name now. Wyatt had asked her if she wanted to tell them or stay incognito. She'd come to like the people in Eagle's Ridge, and it felt wrong to continue to let them think she was Nicole from Virginia, or that she and Wyatt were a thing.

They were definitely not a thing, though she wanted them to be. But she was apparently the only one who did.

His words earlier still rang in her head. That what they

had wasn't important to him. It was sex to him. A fling. They'd had a good time, but it was over. Tomorrow she'd get on her father's plane and head back to Seattle with a new bodyguard. Wyatt wouldn't miss her at all. He had plenty of prospects to replace her in his bed, judging by the women who said hi to him while they walked through the park.

She tried not to think of those things, but she couldn't quite help it. They ran into Claudia again, who said she'd been thinking about what Paige had said and she wanted to talk. Paige would have been excited if not for the ache in her heart that Wyatt had caused. They set a time to talk on the phone, and then Paige and Wyatt moved on.

Diana Wood was there, standing with a tall, somewhat nerdy-looking guy with glasses and a mop of unruly hair. But then they got closer and Paige realized it was August Kensington. He was actually very attractive. There were muscles under that button-down. Quite a lot of them, in fact. The women in her circles in Seattle were always trying to get Augie out on dates, but he was too focused on his tech company to comply. What was he doing in Eagle's Ridge?

"Hello, Augie," Paige said as they got closer.

"Hi, Paige. Where's your father?"

"Still in Seattle, I imagine."

Wyatt seemed a little taken aback. "You two know each other?"

"My dad buys software from Augie's company. You know Augie?"

"We grew up together," Wyatt said.

"That's right," Augie replied. "Born and raised in Eagle's Ridge. I live in Seattle now…" He glanced at Diana, who was smiling at them all politely. "I'm thinking of moving back though. I can run operations from here. And I'd like a change of pace, I think."

"Well," Diana said. "It was lovely to see you again, August. But I need to get going. I promised to meet some friends for dinner."

"Miss Wood," Augie said. "It's always nice to see you."

Paige thought he looked at Diana Wood with the same slack-jawed look Wyatt had given her in Claudia's shop, but then she thought maybe she was wrong. Augie seemed cool and collected. Maybe even oblivious.

Diana glided away in a cloud of elegance in spite of the down-home atmosphere of carnival rides and fried food on sticks. Paige wished she could bottle that and sell it, because she'd make a fortune in no time. They talked to Augie for a bit longer and then he too had to go.

Wyatt introduced her to so many people that she felt like she might never remember them all. There was some laughter over the way everyone had thought she was his ex-girlfriend from Virginia, but Hildie had already disseminated the fact that she'd known all along and had only been helping Wyatt to protect Paige. They even treated the rumors of kissing as if they were part of the cover. After all, Hildie was the only one who'd caught them at it.

They finally caught up with Mary Beth at the horse trailers. The stable had trailered in the horses for the parade, and now they were taking them back again. Zeus was in a trailer munching hay as they walked up, and Mary Beth had changed back into regular shoes with her jods instead of boots. She turned with a smile on her face and opened her arms for Wyatt. He walked into them and gave her a hug, and Paige tried not to let envy get the best of her. Envy because he clearly loved someone, even if that someone wasn't her.

A moment later, Mary Beth patted him on the back and stepped away. Then she opened her arms for Paige.

Paige went into them without even glancing at Wyatt. She wasn't going to let him ruin this for her. She might not know Mary Beth all that well, but she adored the woman. At seventy-eight, Mary Beth was an inspiration. Active, vibrant, and full of fun and sass.

"Did you enjoy the parade, my dears?"

"Yes," Paige replied. "It was lovely. Everything is amazing."

Mary Beth laughed. "Well, I expect you haven't had too many small-town Fourths. I think many of them are the same, but I'm certainly partial to ours. Maybe you'll come back for our fall harvest event."

Paige's throat ached. "I'd like that."

Mary Beth squeezed her hand. "You are welcome anytime. And now, why don't we go and enjoy the carnival? It's a few hours until the fireworks, and we'll want to pick out a good spot."

"Shouldn't you rest for a while, Gran?"

"For heaven's sake, Wyatt, I just rode a horse at a walk for an hour. I don't know how I could get more rested. If we were trotting, different story. But Zeus could put anyone to sleep at a walk."

Wyatt held up both hands. "Fine. Just a suggestion."

"I suggest you stop worrying about me and start having a good time. Paige is leaving us tomorrow. I think we should have fun."

"Yes, ma'am."

"Then let's get the lawn chairs and go find our place."

―――

FUN. It wasn't exactly fun hanging around with Paige and

Gran, watching the two of them laugh and talk like they'd known each other their whole lives. Wyatt trailed behind, carrying the bag chairs on one shoulder and tugging the cooler on wheels. Gran had a bag with a picnic blanket and supplies, but Paige took it from her as they walked.

They found a spot under a tree. Not too far under the tree or they wouldn't see the fireworks. Other people were staking out their spots as well. Gran spread the blanket and Wyatt set up the chairs. Paige unpacked the bag for Gran.

By the time they were done, Gran had produced an entire picnic with cold fried chicken, potato salad, and some sort of marinated vegetable salad. She had wine and acrylic glasses as well as bottles of water and some of her homemade iced tea. Wyatt was surprised that his stomach growled, but it had been hours since they'd eaten barbecue.

"This is amazing, Mary Beth," Paige said. "You thought of everything."

Gran winked. "I even have dessert. Sugar free, of course."

They fixed plates and ate while the sun sank in the sky and people began to pack the area with their own chairs and coolers. Wyatt sat back and watched the activity around him. He'd missed this. It had been years since he'd experienced July Fourth in Sentinel Park. He used to come with Gran and Gramps when he was little. When he was older, he hung out with his friends. They snuck beers and dared each other to do things that would get them in trouble if caught.

Hell, they'd even pranked Augie one year. They'd jammed the door to the portable toilet closed and left him in there for an hour. They'd gotten in pretty big trouble for that one. It was a wonder Augie didn't hold a grudge, but he really didn't. One of the nicest guys you'd meet. And one of the richest.

Wyatt slanted a glance at Paige. Now Augie was the kind of guy she should be hanging out with. Wealthy, self-made. A real self-starter.

The idea of her with Augie made his teeth snap together and grind. Augie Kensington was a great guy, but he wasn't enough of a challenge for Paige. A woman like Paige would walk all over poor Augie.

She sat talking to Gran and laughing about something —but then her face went white and he shot up from his chair, his instincts on high alert as he scanned the crowd.

"What's the matter, dear?" Gran was saying. "Are you feeling okay?"

"I… Yes, I'm fine." Paige smiled and set her plate on the small folding table Gran had managed to pack in that giant bag of hers. "I just… I thought I saw something. It was nothing though."

Wyatt was at her side in half a second, taking a knee beside her and making her look at him. Her eyes were a little wide, a little scared.

"What did you see, Paige?"

"I…" She closed her eyes. "It's nothing. I'm seeing things because I'm still rattled. There was a man… he looked familiar. But it wasn't him. I was mistaken. He couldn't know I was here anyway. I haven't told anyone back home."

Wyatt stood and cast his gaze around the crowd. It was a damned protection nightmare and he'd let himself be led right into it. The crowd was big, it was getting dark, and he had two women he needed to watch, not just one. He couldn't abandon Gran to take care of all this stuff by herself while he escorted Paige out of here.

And he couldn't leave Paige while he went and

searched the crowd. She dug her fingers into his arm and forced him to look at her.

"I was mistaken, Wyatt. Don't get yourself worked up over this. There are so many people here, and I glanced into the crowd and let myself get scared over nothing."

Logically, Joshua Kingsley wouldn't be here. They'd only admitted Paige's identity today—and besides, Kingsley had a restraining order against him. Even if he knew where she was, he'd be crazy to come.

"Maybe we should get out of here. I'll call one of the guys—"

"No. Sit down. Enjoy this with your grandmother. She's made all this food, and she's so happy you're here." She pitched her voice low so Gran couldn't hear.

Gran's attention had been caught by Amy Wells and her toddler. They'd stopped to speak to Gran—or Amy had—and the kid was wearing an Uncle Sam outfit that had Gran exclaiming over him.

"She won't mind," he began.

"Wyatt, listen to me. It means so much to her that you're enjoying this with her. Besides, you're a badass Navy SEAL. Nobody's getting the jump on you."

He looked around again. As much as he hated it, they had to stay until the show was over. The logistics of getting out of here right now were insane. Another half hour and the fireworks were happening. Kids were already lighting up sparklers. Dusk was falling fast, and darkness would be here before he could maneuver them out of traffic and get back up the mountain.

"Don't leave my side, Paige. Not for anything."

"I won't. Not tonight anyway."

Chapter 24

As darkness settled, Paige grew more relaxed. She hadn't really seen Joshua Kingsley. She'd seen a man that reminded her of him. Her imagination was strained because she was so stressed. Stressed that she was leaving tomorrow, that she was in love with Wyatt Chandler, and that he didn't feel the same way.

She kept hoping it would happen. That a lightning bolt would strike him and he'd realize the truth. But he never did. He stayed near her as the fireworks started, but he didn't reach for her hand. At least when he'd been pretending with her, he'd touched her. Now that everyone knew she was a client and not his ex from Virginia, he didn't even make the effort.

She had to wonder if he would spend the night in her bed tonight or if he'd go to his own room and sleep alone.

The fireworks boomed and popped, and the crowd oohed and aahed. The show truly was spectacular. Paige glanced over at Mary Beth, who seemed to be having a good time.

But then Mary Beth put her hand to her heart and grimaced. Paige touched her arm and leaned in.

"Mary Beth, are you okay?"

"I'm fine, honey," she said. "Just a little tired."

But her breath sounded labored. There were beads of sweat on her brow and her skin was cool when Paige touched her. Panic flared.

"Wyatt," she shouted over noise, grabbing his arm and shaking him. He was watching the crowd and the fireworks, but the second she touched him he was on his feet, reaching for his weapon.

He didn't draw though. He was too well trained to draw in this crowd unless absolutely necessary.

"It's your grandmother," she told him.

Mary Beth waved a hand. "I'm fine. Fine."

Paige had been sitting between them, so he hadn't seen his grandmother looking ill. He saw it now. The anguish on his face pierced her to the core.

"Gran," he said, dropping beside her. "What is it? Is it your heart?"

Paige couldn't hear what was said over the fireworks, but several of the people sitting nearby began to get the idea that something was wrong with Mary Beth.

They cleared a circle as Wyatt picked his grandmother up and laid her back on the ground.

"Call 9-1-1!" he shouted. Several people were on their phones in an instant.

Paige backed away to give him room, her heart pounding, tears scalding her throat. Mary Beth couldn't die. She just couldn't. Wyatt would be devastated—and so would she, though not in the same way since she hadn't known his grandmother as long.

Sirens sounded in the distance, and someone said

they'd go and wait for the paramedics on the street so they could direct them to the spot beneath the tree.

Paige dashed tears from her cheeks and watched as Wyatt bent over his grandmother.

No, no, no! This couldn't be happening. It just couldn't.

The paramedics arrived soon after and pushed the crowd aside as they raced to the scene. Paige was thrust farther from the circle. She stumbled but righted herself, catching someone's arm as she did so.

Whoever it was helped her stay on her feet. She didn't have the ability to thank them as she continued to watch the crowd around Mary Beth for signs that she was going to be okay.

But then strong arms went around her and yanked her back against a broad chest. She started to struggle, but something hard and round poked her in the side.

"Don't fight it, my queen."

———

WYATT'S HEART stopped for the few minutes when Gran was prone on the ground, looking pale and deathly ill. But the paramedics arrived and took over from him, and he straightened, his eyes blurred and his heart hammering.

Words floated up to him as they worked on her.

"Diabetic," one of the paramedics said, checking the medical ID bracelet that Gran wore.

"Hypoglycemia," said the other. They worked rapidly, checking Gran's blood levels and then injecting her with something. Then they put her on the gurney and cleared a path.

"We'll need to take her to the hospital for observation," the first paramedic said to him.

"Is she going to be okay?"

Gran was awake, but her breathing was shallow and rapid, and she seemed unaware of what was happening around her.

"She should be. We got to her in time. The doctors can tell you more. If you'd like to ride with us, sir, you can."

"Yeah, I'd like that." He turned to Paige. She wasn't behind him. He scanned the surrounding area. There was no familiar blond head. Knives stabbed at his insides.

The paramedics were already wheeling Gran toward the ambulance. *Shit.*

There was no way he could go with them though. Not without Paige.

Zane and Harper came running up. "We heard something was happening with Mrs. Chandler," Harper said. "Can we help?"

Wyatt had never been so lost in his life. How could he choose? But he had a duty to perform. A duty he took seriously. Gran was okay right now. He had to believe she would stay that way.

"Can you go with her? I have to find Paige. She was here, and now…" *Where* the hell was she?

"We'll go," Zane said. "I'll call you, okay?"

"Thanks, Zane."

Zane squeezed his shoulder. "It'll be all right. Find your girl."

"She's not my girl," Wyatt said as if on autopilot.

Zane gave him a serious look. "Right. I've seen you with her. I know better."

He and Harper took off for the ambulance before it left, and Wyatt began to search for Paige. The park was so jammed it made it difficult to maneuver, but the good part about that was that it would also be difficult to maneuver for Paige and her assailant.

Because there was little doubt in his mind that she'd been taken. Paige wasn't stupid. She wouldn't have left his side. And certainly not when Gran was so ill. The two of them had formed a bond already. She cared about Gran, and she wouldn't take off like this.

The fact she had? It set all his senses to tingling—and that wasn't a good thing at all.

His phone rang and he grabbed it from his pocket. "Chandler."

"I just got word that Joshua Kingsley disappeared off the radar," Hawk said. "He was supposed to check in with the PD this morning, but he missed the appointment. Someone just called me."

Rage rolled through Wyatt like a steam engine. "They *just now* called? He's been missing for hours."

"Yeah, I'm not happy about it. There's no indication Kingsley knows where to find Paige though. He probably ran to avoid the hearing. This isn't the first time he's harassed a woman."

Wyatt's heart throbbed. If he lost Paige now. If he lost her over his own stupidity—

Dammit all to hell, why had he brought her here tonight?

"He's here."

"Kingsley is there? In Eagle's Ridge? Are you certain?"

Wyatt hadn't stopped searching since he'd answered the phone. He was beginning to get frantic as he methodically made his way across the park. "Paige is missing. I'm on the hunt now."

"All right. Shit. I'll see what I can mobilize from this end. Keep me informed."

"Yep, will do."

THE GUN JABBED into her ribs was sobering. Paige had never experienced such a thing in her life. It made her wonder how Wyatt had survived twelve years in the Navy. He'd been a SEAL, fighting terrorists and performing acts of heroism she couldn't begin to imagine. He must have faced down a person with a gun before. How had he done it?

Because she was torn between being a mess and being brave, and she hadn't even seen the gun. Joshua Kingsley kept her moving forward relentlessly. Navigating the crowd was enough of an issue to keep her partly distracted from her dilemma.

Partly. Because the rest of her was fully aware there was a gun in her ribs.

Her eyes still stung with tears over Mary Beth. She had no idea what had happened, but she'd heard the ambulance scream away from the park. She hoped that meant that Mary Beth was alive and headed toward the hospital.

"Paige," a female voice called. "Paige!"

"Keep moving," Joshua growled, "or I'll shoot the bitch."

Paige dashed the tears from her cheeks as she tried to see who had called to her. Maybe they could get a message to Wyatt. Maybe Wyatt would come and save her.

But how could he when he was taking care of Mary Beth?

"Paige!" It was Hildie Fontana who came bustling up to them. Her expression fell when she saw Joshua. He held Paige close, his gun wedged tight to her body. But to Hildie, it probably looked like they were romantic.

"Get rid of her," Joshua said in her ear.

"Hi, Mrs. Fontana. Did you need something?"

Hildie looked a little perplexed. "Well, I heard that Mary Beth had a heart attack. Is it true?"

"I don't know if she did or not. I had to leave."

The gun in her side jabbed harder.

"I mean I'm leaving. I don't know anything. This is my, uh, friend, Joshua. He came to pick me up and take me home."

"Oh, how lovely." Hildie smiled.

"We need to get going," Paige said. "It's a long way back to Seattle."

"Oh, of course. It was so nice meeting you, Paige."

"You too."

Hildie peered around her to Joshua Kingsley. "Pleasure meeting you, young man."

"Yeah, you too," Joshua said. "We've got to get going now. Bye."

Joshua pushed her forward. Hildie didn't stop them, and they started moving through the crowd again.

"You should let me go," Paige said. "Just let me go and get out of here while you can. Nobody knows you're here—"

"Shut up!" He sucked in a breath, as if trying to retain control. "You got me fired. I loved you, and you treated me like dirt! You need to be punished for that. If you're lucky, I'll take you back once you've groveled enough."

"I didn't get you fired," she said, digging down for strength, trying to buy time. Wyatt would save her. He *would*.

Except he'd been pretty preoccupied with Mary Beth.

Oh God, Mary Beth. Please let her be okay.

"You told them to fire me. I couldn't pay my rent. I got evicted."

"I'm sorry, but I swear it wasn't me."

"Rich bitch. Sitting in that fancy penthouse, eating off gold plates and burning hundred-dollar bills while I searched for a place to live. I loved you and you did that to me."

He was unhinged. Seriously unhinged. Panic swelled in Paige's throat as they reached the edge of the park and Joshua shoved her along faster. The crowd was thinner here, so they moved more quickly. Paige tried to think of how to distract him, how to get away, but her mind was blank. She wasn't a commando, had no idea how Wyatt did what he did. She wished she'd asked. He could have taught her self-defense moves, but she'd been too busy thinking about sex with him to think about anything else.

Joshua shoved her through a gap in the bushes, and she stumbled out onto the street. Headlights flared brightly in front of her, and she raised her hands to shield her vision. The car screeched to a halt and the driver yelled something, but she didn't know what because Joshua pushed her across the street and jerked her onto the sidewalk.

He finally stopped beside a beat-up old Jeep and wrapped his arm—the one with the gun—around her throat while he reached for the keys to unlock the vehicle. Paige sucked in her breath and told herself to *think*. Just think. The gun wasn't trained on her now. If she could stomp his instep or kick him in the groin, maybe she could buy enough time to get away.

Paige lifted her foot, ready to slam it down. But she was jerked backward before she could do it. She thought maybe he'd realized what was happening, but instead they were falling. She reached out, tried to catch herself, but she hit the concrete with a hard thud. Her face bounced against the rough sidewalk, her cheek taking the brunt of the blow.

Her brain told her to get up. Get moving. Run while she could. She pushed herself over onto her stomach so she could lift her body and run. Joshua wasn't holding her, but she didn't know when he'd grab her again, and she didn't want to be there when he tried. He must have lost his balance somehow. Maybe he'd hit his head harder than she'd hit her face and he was knocked out for a few moments.

Paige got to her feet, her knees and face hurting, her hands stinging from the scramble to get upright. That's when she saw Joshua. He was on his feet, his eyes wide, his throat exposed as his head was wrenched back.

Someone had a hand in his hair and a gun against his cheek.

"Wyatt!"

He glanced at her. His eyes were hard, cold. Determined. Her heart throttled into the danger zone.

"Don't come any closer, Paige."

Joshua's nostrils flared as he started to curse. "I'm going to kill you both," he spat out.

"Oh really?" Wyatt asked. He sounded gleeful. Like he was looking for an excuse to unleash his rage. "You're going to kill us both, huh? When will that be?"

Joshua's eyes gleamed as they landed on her. "You've disappointed me, my queen. I thought you were pure. The one. You're nothing but trash. You have to be sacrificed."

He still had the keys in his hand. He lifted them and pressed something. There was a click. An audible click from behind her. Paige turned.

Wyatt shouted something. She didn't hear what, precisely, because she was focused on that click. It wasn't the doors unlocking. It wasn't anything she'd ever heard.

"Paige, *run!*"

Belatedly, her brain kicked into gear and she started to do as Wyatt ordered. Her skinned knees screamed in pain, but she shoved one foot in front of the other as hard as she could. Her breath razored in, her heart pounded like mad, and her legs churned.

But it wasn't quite enough. There was a blast—and then she was thrown into the air, screaming. She came down on top of a car—and everything went holy-shit black.

Chapter 25

Wyatt clawed his way to his feet and ran toward where he'd last seen Paige. Flames leaped from Joshua Kingsley's Jeep, climbing into the air and threatening the trees overhead. Kingsley's body lay on the sidewalk. Unmoving. A piece of metal jutted from his throat as blood pooled around him.

Wyatt couldn't spare any time for the scumbag. His body ached from where he'd dived behind a cement planter. It had sheltered him from the blast. But if the explosion had been any stronger, it would have been lights out for him as well.

He skidded to a halt two cars away. Paige lay partly on the roof, partly on the trunk and back window. The glass had spider-webbed but not broken. She was still. Too still.

He couldn't move her in case her back was broken, but he checked her pulse. It was still beating. He checked for rapidly filling pools of blood.

There were none. Her cheek was scraped up from where she'd hit the concrete earlier, but she wasn't bleeding out.

Didn't mean she wasn't bleeding internally. She'd been thrown into the air and then come down hard on this car.

Inside, he was a shaking, screaming mess. Outside, he went into commando mode and stayed there.

Please, please, please.

"Paige, baby, are you with me? Can you hear me?"

In the distance, sirens flared and screamed. Vaguely, he heard the shouts of people across the street in the park. A crowd would be headed this way in about two seconds.

"Wyatt." Her voice was barely a whisper.

He bent down to her. He wanted to drag her into his arms and hold her, but he couldn't risk that. He had to leave her like this until the paramedics arrived. He was trained in combat medicine, of course. But they were coming and they had the proper equipment. He had to let them get here and do their jobs.

Gran flitted through his mind, and a wave of nausea hit him in the gut. Gran and Paige. The two women he adored. Both could be dying, and there was nothing he could do.

He hadn't protected them at all. He'd tried, but he hadn't.

Paige reached out and fisted a hand in his T-shirt. It was a surprisingly strong grip. That gave him a measure of hope.

"Not your fault, Wyatt. Don't go there."

He blinked. How the hell did she know what he was thinking?

"I should have taken better care of you," he said, his face close to hers. He stroked her hair, kissed her forehead. If he lost her—

God, he couldn't think like that. He just couldn't.

"No," she said, her voice a little stronger now. "You did your job. You did everything you were supposed to."

He didn't feel like he had. Not at all. He'd gotten distracted in the park with Gran, and he'd let that take precedence over protecting Paige. But hell, what could he have done differently? Gran had been critical, and Paige had been fine.

Until she wasn't there anymore. Until Joshua Kingsley had gotten to her.

"I let him get you. I'm sorry."

"You couldn't know. You had to take care of Mary Beth. Is she…" She swallowed. "What happened?"

"She's at the hospital. She was stable when they took her."

Paige closed her eyes. "Thank God."

Yes, thank God was right.

There was nothing else he could say at that moment because a police cruiser came roaring up, blue lights blazing bright. Lieutenant Michael Stonecipher climbed out. Another cruiser arrived, and the police started clearing the gathering crowd. A fire truck burst onto the scene and blasted the burning Jeep with water. It hissed like a demon before subsiding just as the ambulance screeched up. Paramedics piled from the interior with their bags and gurneys.

"Don't leave me," Paige gasped as the paramedics swarmed.

"I won't," Wyatt said, gripping her hand. "I promise I won't."

And he wouldn't. Not ever again.

———

PAIGE WOKE IN A STRANGE PLACE. It took her a moment, listening to the beeps and whirrs, before she remembered being lifted onto a gurney and slipped into the back of an ambulance. Wyatt had been with her, but now…?

She tried to sit up, groaning as pain radiated through her limbs. Firm hands pushed gently on her shoulders.

"Don't move, baby. You're going to be sore for a while."

She blinked up at the face hovering over her. "Wyatt?"

"Yeah, it's me."

The smile he gave her was tired and maybe a little uncertain. Her heart dropped. Not for herself, though she felt like hell, but for Mary Beth. Because that's the only reason he'd be upset, right?

"Mary Beth?" she croaked.

He reached for a giant lidded cup with a straw. "You thirsty?"

"Yes."

She lifted her head and he guided the straw to her lips so she could drink.

"Mary Beth," she said a moment later, her throat moist again. "How is she?"

Wyatt threaded his fingers in hers and squeezed. "She's going to be okay. It wasn't a heart attack at all. Her blood sugar got too low and she didn't realize it. The doc explained to me that it happens to diabetics sometimes. They don't know it's happening because they don't feel anything until it hits. She's lucky we were there. We got her help fast, and that's probably what saved her life. If she'd gone into a diabetic coma at home alone… well, that wouldn't have been good."

Relief washed through her. She was already weak from whatever drugs they were giving her, but the relief intensified the effect. *Thank God Mary Beth was well.*

Wyatt brought her hand to his mouth and pressed his lips there. "I'm sorry I didn't protect you better."

"It wasn't your fault, Wyatt." Stubborn man! How many times did she have to tell him? "You did everything you could—and you helped me find out who was stalking me in the first place. Without you, who knows what might have happened?"

His eyes gleamed in the low light of the room. "You don't really believe that, do you? I screwed up when I turned my back on you—no, I screwed up when I failed to get you out of there when you thought you saw him earlier. Because you *did* see him."

Paige thought back to that moment, that flash in the crowd. It had happened so fast that she'd convinced herself she was wrong. Logically, she'd had to be. That's what she'd thought anyway.

"I didn't know what I saw. And I've been on edge since I identified him, so I thought I was being paranoid." She closed her eyes. "What happened? I still don't quite know how you got there, or how I fell. And then the click—what was that?"

Wyatt took a deep breath, let it out. He shoved a hand through his hair. He did not let go of her hand.

"As soon as I knew you were missing, I started looking for you. It was Hildie Fontana who pointed me in the right direction. She called me and told me she'd just seen you and you didn't look right. She was following you, Paige. She told me where to go, and I did."

Paige couldn't believe it. But the next time she saw Hildie, she was giving the woman a giant hug. And buying something hugely expensive from her shop.

"As for your fall… I'm sorry, but that's my fault too. I had to act before Kingsley realized I was there. When I grabbed him, it took you off-balance too."

His fingers skimmed over her cheek. It felt funny, so she

reached up and discovered the tape there. Tape for her injuries.

"You'll have some scarring," he said. "But it will fade in a few months, according to the doctor. The cuts aren't severe."

Scarring? She gulped. But hey, she was alive, and she owed that to Wyatt and Hildie apparently. That was far more important than scarring. She'd deal with that when it happened.

"What about the click?"

"Do you remember the explosion?"

Paige searched her memory, but it wouldn't come. She remembered everything up to the click. Then she remembered being put into the ambulance with Wyatt at her side.

"No."

Wyatt squeezed her hand again. "The click was a bomb, honey. Joshua Kingsley had wired a bomb to his Jeep. I don't know what he meant to do—maybe he intended to kill you both should the cops catch up to him."

Horror filled her. "A bomb?"

"It didn't detonate right away. I told you to run, and you did. But you were caught in the blast and thrown into the air. You landed on a car. You didn't break anything, but you're going to be sore for a good long while."

"I landed on a car? How did you survive? And what about Joshua?"

"I dived behind a cement planter. The blast wasn't a very strong one, but strong enough to throw you. A piece of shrapnel lodged into Joshua Kingsley's throat—he didn't survive."

Paige could hardly process it all. There'd been a bomb. She'd been thrown into the air. Joshua Kingsley was dead. But Wyatt was here and he was alive. Mary Beth was going to be well. A tear leaked down her cheek. Wyatt wiped it away.

"I'm not crying about him," she whispered.

"I know."

"I'm just relieved—that you're okay, that Mary Beth is recovering, that I'm alive."

"Yeah, it's been a helluva night. But we're all going to be okay."

"I'm not going back to Seattle tomorrow," she said firmly. Because she loved this man, and she was going to stay here and fight for him. She'd figure out the rest later. Somehow she'd make him see that he had to give them a chance.

"No, you aren't ready to go anywhere."

She squeezed his hand. "That's not what I mean, Wyatt. I mean I'm not going, not until you and I have a long talk about some things."

"What kind of things?"

He regarded her with what might be amusement, but she wasn't certain. She gulped down her fear and decided to put it all out there. Heart on the line. Go for it. It's what successful people did—they fought for what they wanted.

"Us. You and me."

"And Mr. Fluffypants?"

She blinked. "Well, yes. He's part of the deal."

"I'm going to save you the trouble, Paige. We're going to figure it out, because there is definitely an us. I can't leave Eagle's Ridge, not permanently—especially not now that Gran has had an episode—but I can fly to Seattle for a few days from time to time. And you can fly here. We'll figure it out."

Her heart monitor began to beep more frequently as her heart rate increased.

"What are you saying, Wyatt?"

"I'm saying I want to be with you. That I'm crazy for you. That when I thought I'd lost you, I felt the kind of soul-crushing despair I'd never felt before. You rock my world, Paige Spencer. You and your ridiculous feline. I love being with you, talking with you. I've told you things I never told anyone—and you made me think about it in a different way than I have before. I can't imagine letting you go without telling you these things. Without telling you that I think I'm in love with you."

Joy swelled inside her. "I think I'm in love with you too."

His smile was broad. It lit her world. "Then I think we're going to have to figure this love thing out together, don't you?"

<hr>

ONE MONTH LATER...

"BABE, HAVE YOU SEEN MY SOCK?"

Paige looked up from her computer. "Sock? You're missing a sock?"

"Yeah," Wyatt said. "I put a pair on the bed for when I got out of the shower. One's missing."

She screwed up her pretty lips. He loved that look. It was her serious thinking look. "Oh my goodness," she said, jumping to her feet and rushing toward the laundry room.

Wyatt padded after her, curious. When he reached the room, she was bent down and staring into the cat's litter box. Wyatt began to get a bad feeling about the fate of his sock.

"The little bastard buried it, didn't he?"

Paige spun as she stood. Her hand popped over her

mouth. He didn't miss the giggle she tried to hide. "I'm afraid he did," she finally said.

Wyatt dropped his head even as he shook it. "That cat hates me."

Paige rushed over and put her arms around his waist. His groin began to perk up at the close proximity of her lush body.

"He doesn't, I promise! He's just mischievous. He's testing you."

"He's been testing me since he met me."

"Yes, but he's never crapped in your bed again, has he?"

"No, but that's because we sleep together. And he loves you."

Paige laughed. He pretended to be insulted, but he really wasn't. He loved her laugh.

"He'll settle down soon, I promise. So long as you don't let him chase you away."

"Let a rat bastard of a cat keep me from you? No, not happening." He held her loosely. His groin was definitely showing signs of interest now. And she would soon know it.

"Oh my," she said after a couple more seconds. "Is that a gun in your pocket, or are you happy to see me?"

"Always happy to see you." He dipped his lips to her throat, dragged in the sweet scent of her as he kissed her skin. "Always happy to taste you."

Her arms looped around his neck. "Did you forget you were showering because we have dinner plans with Mary Beth?"

Shit.

"No, of course not." He sighed and took a step back. "Guess I'd better find another pair of socks."

"Guess so."

She followed him to the bedroom where he dug in the

dresser for socks. They didn't live far from Gran, but they still had to pick her up. And they had reservations at Blue Moon.

They were celebrating a few things. First, Paige's partnership with Claudia over at the boutique. Paige had bought the building from the owner, and she'd been helping Claudia redesign the store and order in merchandise, including some of her own designs. Poor Claudia had been beside herself when she realized it was her excited post about meeting Paige on a fan board for *American Princess* that had helped Joshua Kingsley find her. She'd cried so hard that Paige had hugged her tight and told her it wasn't her fault.

Wyatt had been angry, but he'd had to reluctantly agree. Claudia was a sweet soul, and she hadn't thought she was doing wrong. She'd never mentioned that Paige was in Eagle's Ridge, but Claudia's profile indicated where she lived. Kingsley followed the boards for information about Paige, and he'd lucked onto the post. He'd put two and two together and headed for Eagle's Ridge.

American Princess had been canceled, but Paige swore she didn't want to return to it anyway. She'd started her video channel, and she was getting interest from viewers. Eventually she'd build her brand into the juggernaut she wanted it to be. He had complete faith in her.

The other thing they were celebrating was his new security firm, Chandler Protective Services. He'd recruited a couple of guys from his military days, and they'd signed on to protect Greg Spencer and some of his corporate managers when they showed up for a business trip next week. He'd also gotten interest for public events, like the upcoming Fall Bash.

The last thing they were celebrating was Gran's continued good health. Since her episode on July Fourth, she'd been hypervigilant about checking her blood sugar. Wyatt hadn't wanted to let her move back home alone, but she'd insisted. She'd promised him she wouldn't let an episode like that one happen again. She'd been so wrapped up in the parade and the celebration that she hadn't eaten enough. When her blood sugar dropped, she didn't notice the signs until it was too late.

But now she was on guard, and the doctor had given her a prescription for something in case she felt like it was happening again. Wyatt had intended to stay in the apartment over the garage for a while longer. Paige had been completely on board.

Gran had refused. She said that a couple nurturing a new romance didn't need to live with an old lady. And then she'd said she didn't want to hear any noises coming from the bedroom.

Wyatt had actually blushed over that one, but Paige had laughed and said no problem, they'd find a place close by. And they had. A cute little rental house a street over. Eventually they'd look for a more permanent place—but not until he was certain Gran was going to be fine.

Wyatt put on his socks, shoved on his shoes—dress shoes, which he didn't much like—and spread his arms. "Work for you?"

"Baby, everything about you works for me," Paige said.

"Careful with those eyes, or we'll be late."

She snorted. "Can't control yourself?"

"Not when you look at me like that." He let his gaze slide down the little black dress she wore. She had those high heels with the red bottoms on again. He loved the way they made her legs look. He really loved it when she kept them on and wrapped her legs around his waist. "Better get out to the car, Paige. Or I won't be responsible for my actions."

She laughed and dashed toward the door. He followed. He could catch her, but he let himself enjoy her ass instead. Still, when they got outside and she stood beside the truck, waiting for him to unlock it, he pressed her against the door and kissed her hotly.

"I love you," he growled against her lips.

"I know," she said, lifting her arms around his neck. "Best thing that ever happened to me, by the way."

"Nah," he told her very seriously. "The best is yet to come."

And it was. Life with Paige was more exciting and satisfying than he'd ever dreamed. He couldn't wait to see what came next...

Also by Lynn Raye Harris

The Hostile Operations Team Books

The HOT SEAL Team Books

Book 1: HOT SEAL - Dane & Ivy

Book 2: HOT SEAL Lover - Remy & Christina

Book 3: HOT SEAL Rescue - Cody & Miranda

Book 4: HOT SEAL BRIDE - Coming Soon!

The HOT Novella in Liliana Hart's MacKenzie Family Series

HOT WITNESS - Jake & Eva

7 Brides for 7 Brothers

MAX (Book 5) - Max & Ellie

About the Author

Lynn Raye Harris is the *New York Times* and *USA Today*
bestselling author of the HOSTILE OPERATIONS
TEAM SERIES of military romances as well as twenty
books for Harlequin Presents. A former finalist for the
Romance Writers of America's Golden Heart Award and
the National Readers Choice Award, Lynn lives in
Alabama with her handsome former-military husband, two
crazy cats, and one spoiled American Saddlebred horse.
Lynn's books have been called "exceptional and emotion-
al," "intense," and "sizzling." Lynn's books have sold over
three million copies worldwide.

To connect with Lynn online:

www.LynnRayeHarris.com
Lynn@LynnRayeHarris.com